MW00911898

Itsy 'BITS'y Tales
Pilani in the 80's

Itsy 'BITS'y Tales
Pilani in the 80's

Terence Alvares
Batch of 1983

BLACK EAGLE BOOKS
2020

BLACK EAGLE BOOKS

USA address:
7464 Wisdom Lane
Dublin, OH 43016

India address:
E/312, Trident Galaxy, Kalinga Nagar,
Bhubaneswar-751003, Odisha, India

E-mail: info@blackeaglebooks.org
Website: www.blackeaglebooks.org

First International Edition published by
Black Eagle Books, 2020

Itsy 'BITS'y Tales Pilani in the 80's
by Terence Alvares (Batch of 1983)

Copyright © **Terence Alvares**

All rights reserved. No part of this publication may be reproduced, stored in a retrieval system, or transmitted, in any form or by any means, electronic, mechanical, photocopying, recording or otherwise without the prior permission of the publisher.

Cover & Interior Design: Ezy's Publication

ISBN- 978-1-64560-126-5 (Paperback)
Library of Congress Control Number: 2020949082

Printed in United States of America

Pilani in the 1980's

BITS Pilani was and remains one of India's premier educational Institutions. The campus is in the remote North corner of Rajasthan in India and in the 80's, was about a 5-hour bus trip from Jaipur or Delhi. These were the main transit points for students who came from all over the country. Excepting a few faculty and staff kids, all the students lived in hostels. At that time there were 11 boys' hostels and one girls' hostel, called bhawans. Each student had a room to themselves. Each bhawan housed about 200 students. So, the boy to girl ratio on campus was about 11:1 and this gender imbalance, along with the remoteness from a big town or city, played out in interesting ways in the campus social scene.

The campus had an auditorium that could seat about 2000 people. It hosted two movies each weekend: one English and one Hindi. These were the highlights of one's week. Next to the main Institute building is Skylab, with beautifully manicured lawns and a kiosk run by 'Pappu'. It was a popular hangout between classes. In the evening people would hang out at a mini shopping centre called Shiv Ganga market, more well known as C'Not after the iconic Delhi market. Others would visit Nutan market, which was at the interstate bus stand just outside the campus. There were also a couple of street food carts (rehris) that visited the campus. 2-minute Maggi noodles were cooked in rooms and a ready replacement for missed mess food.

There is a beautiful Saraswati temple on campus and its lawns were a popular hangout place as well in the evenings. Next to Meera Bhawan was a residential girls school called Birla Balika Vidyapeeth. There was also a Science Museum and a gliding club on campus.

Outside the campus was Pilani town. At that time the town had very little to offer except a movie theatre called Dubba and a place called Nihali Chowk, where students visited for different reasons. A bit has changed over the years, I hear. I was a student there more than 30 years ago and haven't been there since.

Getting admission to BITS Pilani was an accomplishment and for a lot of people a transformation. Students were in control of studies and social life; unlike school, no parents or relatives or teachers monitoring them. They could choose their instructors; attendance to class wasn't compulsory. This was the time before mobile phones, internet and e-mail, social media, and even PCs. The Information Processing Centre (IPC) housed an IBM 1130 machine. One typed in code on punch cards, gave it to an operator, who processed it at night and then gave you a printout with all the errors next day.

One wrote letters to parents, got money by money orders, stood in a queue at the bank to deposit and withdraw money, read the news on next day's newspaper, watched TV (Doordarshan) in a hostel common room; the most popular programs being Chitrahaar and cricket matches

A different time...

Pilani Slang used in this book

Audi	Auditorium
Backie	Person in the room behind in the hostel
Bhawan	Hostel. The boy's hostels were: Shankar, Vyas, Krishna Gandhi, Vishwakarma, Bhagirath, Rana Pratap, Ashok, Ram, Budh, Malviya. The girl's hostel was Meera Bhawan.
Bogs	Bathrooms
Choms	People from Rajasthan
Compree	Comprehensive Exams at the end of term
Dhobi	Washerman/launderer
GKW	Ghas Katney Waali: village women who cut grass in the lawns and in between bhawans. They used sickles.
Golts	People from Andhra Pradesh (which at that time included Telangana)
Illad	A person from Tamil Nadu
Moodas	Chairs made of cane
Nimboli	Neem tree fruit
Rehri	Fast food cart
Shikhanji	A drink made with squeezed limes, with ice and salt and pepper
Sidee	Person living in the next room
Wingee	People living in the same wing in a bhawan

Introduction

The BITS Pilani 1983 batch celebrated its silver jubilee reunion a few years back. A Google Group was formed and batchmates got in touch with each other after 25 years. Later, a WhatsApp group was also formed and is quite vibrant even now.

The stories and snippets published in this collection were my contributions on these Google and WhatsApp groups. They are largely fictional, with varying degrees of real incidents. The places and the environment in Part 1 are in Pilani. The snippets in Part 2 are placed after the batch graduated and based on bits and pieces batchmates shared on google group. They are heavily embellished with my 'creative' imagination, and I've tried to connect them with our Pilani times. The 'Pilani' way remains in all of us even after all these years. All character names have been changed and if there is any resemblance to anyone, it is purely unintentional.

One name is real though. I am dedicating this book to my close friend Vivek Marwaha (Cookie).

My contributions on the Google and WhatsApp groups fired up memories among our batchmates. A little after the batch silver jubilee meet, Vivek Marwaha began a battle with cancer. Vivek would look forward to reading my next story each morning. I would call him later in the day and get 'feedback'. That motivated me to continue writing. Unfortunately, Vivek lost his battle a few years ago. I am using his name with permission from his wife. The Vivek stories, like the others, are mostly fiction. Vivek didn't mind when I wrote them.

We came to Pilani in 1983, fresh out of school after years of hard work preparing for Year XII exams and entrance exams. Most of us had lived sheltered lives. Pilani was independence. It was time to explore relationships and build great friendships.

BITS was, and is, a centre of academic excellence with its graduates leading top organisations across the globe. This book however is not about academics. It's all about campus life and real and imaginary friendships, encounters, romances, relationships and experiences.

Our batch, as with other BITS batches, is unanimous in its opinion that these were some of the best years of our lives. Living on campus for a term (four and a half months) at a time, away from family, we built close friendships and continue to stay in touch.

■

Acknowledgements

I would like to thank Sridhar Parthasarathy for spending endless hours proofreading the contents of this book; overriding my emotional conversational style with the dictates of proper grammar and punctuation. VK Raghavan has contributed the sketches of the campus. Sanjay Uppal has contributed photographs he took at our time in Pilani. Vivek Marwaha had been an inspiration when I first wrote these snippets giving me daily feedback. Rajnish Babbar has organised the cover page. Needless to say, these are all my batchmates.

I would also like to thank the whole BITS 83 batch who engaged with my stories all through. I have enjoyed writing them.

I treasure my time at Pilani and this group of friends and batchmates. I always will.

Epilogue

Last Day at Pilani

He had slept well. Last night, he had found an Old Monk bottle under his bed with a peg or two. He had sat on the short armchair in the deserted balcony and gulped it down.

His alarm had gone off at 6:00am. Quick shower, he packed his bedding and the last of his clothes. He went to the mess at 7:00 am. He was the first one there. He had his regular 'French toast', some lukewarm tea and by force of habit walked up to Giri the mess servant for a cigarette. He had cleared his account the previous night (Giri had ensured that) and paid for the last cigarette. He said bye to Giri his favourite mess servant and Khem Singh the assistant mess manager.

At the door of the mess he paused.

So many mixed memories of food, more fond memories of the company. The mess servants, some of whom he knew well, continued with their work. Another semester, new people, their life wouldn't change much.

Most of his friends had finished exams early and had already left. He'd most probably never see them again.

He walked straight to Nutan bus stand, bought a pack of cigarettes, haggled with a rickshaw wallah and rode back with him to collect his stuff from his room at Ashok Bhawan. He loaded the suitcases and bedding on to the rickshaw and walked alongside the rickshaw to Nutan.

He looked wistfully at the deserted gym, the empty grounds, the silent courts and walked on. He had come to Pilani as a puny, sheltered, shy, scared 18-year-old. Four years later he was leaving a man; having acquired a degree, some vices and some virtues. He had also made memories and friends for life.

Passing the swimming pool, he paused.

He had learnt to swim there, the strong smell of chlorine lingered.

And the girls. He had watched them from 108 Ashok, ride to and from the swimming pool... Sigh!

He walked past the main gates, to the bus stand. The bus was already there. He bought his tickets, got his luggage on and got to his seat...an aisle seat.

The bus started. Through the grimy windows and past the heads of fellow passengers, he had last fleeting glimpses of the place which had been home for the past three and a half years.

He wanted to hold on, time to slow down.

The bus kept moving and gathered speed.

Part 1

PILANI

First Flight

First week of August 1987

She walks from Nutan bus stand towards the campus with a new 'Hero Cycles' ladies' cycle. Her dad walks besides her. She is wearing a 'half sari' and pig tails. Dad asks her to start riding. She says, "Wait, let's enter the campus."

Rickshaws with students arriving on campus whiz past. Groups of guys going to Nutan for chai head the other way.

They look at her. 'Fresher' written all over her. They look at the bike. 'New' written all over it with the cardboard wrappings around the pipe frame.

She enters the campus. Father asks her: "Now?" She says: "A bit further." Father: "You want me to push the bike?"

She: "No."

At the corner of Ashok Bhawan, she is ready.

She halts at the kerb, checks the brakes, straddles the bike, right leg ready to propel.

Dad is holding the 'carrier' at the back. She asks him to let go. She looks ahead. The street is clear. She pushes ahead. The bike wobbles a bit. Dad tries to run after it to catch the carrier again.

She settles down. She is now riding confidently. Dad has a beaming smile on his face. She does a U turn at the next crossing (Shankar-Gandhi) and comes back towards dad. Both father and daughter exchange smiles. She dismounts, and they continue walking towards Meera Bhawan (MB).

No more apprehension. The girl has learnt to fly!

The guy in 108 Ashok applauds 'silently'.

II.

It's two weeks into the term. Her dad has gone back. She has sent four letters in these two weeks and received two herself plus a parcel. She misses home.

It's a Sunday afternoon. After lunch, she has cleaned her bike. She heads off to Nutan to fill air in the tyres. It's hot and dusty. She rides back into a sleepy campus; or so she thought.

As she rides past Ashok, she hears shouting, and something hits her front wheel. The impact is not heavy, but the shouting unnerves her, and she wobbles.

The guys in the Ashok upstairs wing, dressed in white Pyjamas-Kurtas are arguing loudly. The only word she can understand is 'Out'. Some North Indians are playing wing cricket. In the wing downstairs, Tall Dutta is walking in the veranda in a cream(ish) singlet and a skimpy, frayed, checked, towel, sashaying his way sleepily to the bogs, soap dish in hand.

By the time she stabilises her steed (bike), she is near Bhagirath Bhawan. She dismounts to check what hit her bike. There is a tennis ball lodged in the spokes of her front wheel. She puts the bike on its stand and dislodges the ball.

KV guy is walking past with his unruly mop of hair, staring at an empty pack of Wills Navy Cut in his hands, muttering to himself: "One day I will be a Principal Software Engineer for a multinational. Then I can buy my own cigarettes."

Jonty comes jogging past, jumps over the barbed wire fence, and runs to his room, he is late for his meeting with 'Honey'...

She tosses the ball over the fence on the gym side and takes off. "Weird People"! she mutters under her breath.

Cookie is practising his tennis on the gym wall, dressed in white shorts, white T shirt, white shoes.... quite Wimbledonesque…

Suddenly, he sees this 'new' tennis ball bouncing across to him. He looks around and sees no one.

Jimmy is coming out of the gym; he finds Cookie staring at the sky. Jimmy asks Cookie: "Kya ho raha hai?" (What is happening?)

Cookie says: "I came from my room with two balls, now I have three!"

III.

As she lay in bed that night, she thought: "Why do I want to be an engineer?"

Lying in her crisp cotton nightie, she looked beyond the coconut oil bottle on her windowsill at the clear night sky. They had said "Shoot for the Stars, and, at worst, you should land on the Moon!"

She thought about the guy with the unruly mop of hair talking to the Wills Navy cut packet, she thought about the guy leaping over the barbed wire fence, she thought about the guy in a cream(ish) singlet and skimpy, frayed, checked towel walking to the bogs, she thought about the guy with the three balls staring at the sky...

She thought to herself: "Why do I want to be an engineer?"

IV.

She woke up with a start. She had a test today and the Favre-Leuba alarm clock hadn't gone off. She jumped up and checked the time. It was just 6.00 am.

Her sidee from the 83 batch, a girl from UP, was up and about, singing mathematical dohas.

She lay back in bed. The first rays of the sun fell on the two posters she had on her wall: Rajnikant and Chiranjeevi. She thought Chiranjeevi winked at her; no, it was just a shadow of the tree branch outside her window.

Gosh...this UP girl was loud! Soon the Balika Vidyapeeth band would start practising; time to wake-up.

She thought about the breakfast coming up: a blob of jam; with a slice of butter with some droplets of water still on it; a much-used steel plate; watery coffee in a jug. Oh, for the pleasures of steaming idlis and crisp dosas...

She went out to the balcony; someone passed her by, looking lovingly at her HMT Asha watch. She looked over the balcony wall and saw her cycle parked downstairs, proudly perched on its stand, handle slanted at a jaunty angle...a la Rajnikant: Mind It!

V.

She said: "My head hurts" and walked away.

An hour ago…

She was invited by a group of seniors to the C'Not shopping centre. Students congregated here after Institute hours at the open-air fast food restaurants. It was her first time. They were walking, so she decided to leave her bike behind. As they left the MB gate she looked back wistfully at her bike and whispered a silent 'Bye…will be back soon".

As she walked, the seniors spoke about the last movie in the Audi, about someone who was in trouble with the warden, about EEE D courses, etc.

As they reached and sat down in C'Not, the talk drifted to various random topics. The group of guys from Ashok Bhawan beside them were still arguing about who lost the ball and should pay for a new one. The guy with the mop of hair who talked to himself was sitting in a corner blowing smoke rings. It seemed like he had found the money to buy cigarettes. The smoke smelt different though.

Her own group started talking about the meaning of life, truth, religion and other abstract stuff. It became quite animated with names of philosophers, quotes and pompous sounding terms being used.

She tried to distract herself by looking at the eagles circling overhead; it didn't work.

She stood up and said: "My head hurts" and walked away…

It was a long lonely walk to MB, but she was relieved. She walked past her bike, lovingly patting the seat and went up to her room. Snoring sounds were emitting from Room 208.

She took the little key she had hidden in her pencil case; pulled out her blue Safari suitcase from under her bed and unlocked it.

Under the pink towel, she found the bottle she was looking for. She unscrewed the top, looked for a steel glass, couldn't find one, took a long drink from the bottle, looked up to Rajnikanth and Chiranjeevi staring at her and sighed…Ah Old Monk!

Her head hurt no more…

VI.

She woke up with a hangover and looked at Rajnikanth. He looked the same whether it be morning or evening....no empathy! She needed to find someone new.

She could hear the noises from the mess and the smell of woodfire. Another day...Sigh!

She decided to go for an early morning bike ride to clear her head. Someone with an 'Appu' watch on one hand and an expensive Casio on the other jogged past in the corridor.

She got on to her bike and took off. The air was crisp. It was foggy. She knew she should slow down, but she just wanted to ride out the hangover. She turned around the temple bend, narrowly avoiding a rickshaw and some GKWs (local women labourers who cut grass with sickles). She bowed slightly as she passed the temple.

She whizzed past Pras as he swayed in his bell bottoms, reading Harry Potter, as he walked to the temple...and then disaster struck.

As she rounded the bend next to Vyas, she crashed into this hairy guy in white pyjamas, who was walking looking at the ground, counting on his fingers.9.1, 9.2,9.3....

Her front wheel stopped between his legs. He screamed, which soon turned into a squeal. He stopped at 9.5!

As she extracted her front wheel from between his legs, she checked her mudguard. It was bent. She looked angrily at this hairy apparition in white.

He was quiet, though his face was a myriad of unspoken painful expressions. She thought to herself:" Here my new bike is damaged, and this guy is concerned about...don't know what...maybe his pyjamas!!!"

VII.

Mr Hairy Pyjamas slowly hobbled away towards Vyas. He walked funny. She suddenly worried whether she had done him some permanent damage. After all the mudguard on her bike could be replaced. She wanted to call out after him, but he was gone, painfully climbing the steps at the Vyas Bhawan entrance.

She saw a cyclist coming out of the mist and stopping by her. Her heart skipped a beat.

Here he was: tall, handsome in an earthy kind of way, close cropped hair. He wore a faded light blue half sleeve shirt. It looked like a school uniform shirt; he had overgrown it. His arms rippled with muscles. The jeans were faded, acid-wash rolled up slightly at his ankles.

His eyes looked through her, as if looking into her soul. She blushed. She regretted not dressing up this morning. Maybe a little coconut oil and some flowers in her hair from the temple lawns...

He parked his bike and bent down to look at her bike. He held the mudguard in his right palm and bent it gently back into shape. Seemed like new! What power in those hands!!

He looked back at her and shyly smiled. She smiled back. He introduced himself. She was too dazed...just caught snatches of it...Haryana....Sports School...going to Gliding Club...and then he got onto his bike and was gone. She kept looking at him as he rounded the bend near Vyas going to C'Not. He disappeared into the fog.

She wondered whether it was a dream.

She knew then who was going to replace Chiranjeevi and Rajnikanth on her wall.

VIII.

She got onto her bike again and slowly pedalled back to MB. The fog had cleared. The lukewarm glow of the morning sun brought a radiance to her face. Her heart was still beating fast. There was a different warmth in her; quite different from the Old Monk!

She rode through a puddle on the road. Another day she would have avoided it to protect her bicycle. Today, she didn't care.

She suddenly remembered she had a class at 8.00 am. No time for breakfast! She parked outside MB, rushed up to her room to collect her books.

She ignored Chiranjeevi and Rajnikanth. She bumped the

'Appu/Casio' jogger who was returning from her jog all sweaty and puffed up. She didn't notice, just ran down the stairs.

She would catch a muffin and coffee through the Skylab 'drive through' on the way to class; maybe get a seat in the last row and eat through class. There was a guy in the Budh front wing who waved as she rode past. He didn't know that the Chief Warden was in his front lawns watching him, waving at her. She didn't care.

It was going to be a long day.

IX.

It was lunchtime. She wasn't hungry. It was too hot to ride back to MB anyway. Her next class was two hours away.

She sat in the corridor next to the ACB office in the M Block. She had been there on her first day.

Today there were some people with dejected faces going in and out. She wondered why. She thought the ACB Dean was a nice guy; he looked like her father.

She thought about her bike. She should check whether it was parked in the shade.

As she sat in the corridor, he legs dangling playfully off the balcony; her mind turned to the guy who fixed up her bike that morning. Would she ever run into him again?

Smiling to herself, playing with her braids, humming a Mylie Cyrus song, someone called out: "Fresher?"

Startled, she turned and looked behind. There was this guy in jeans, kurta and chappals looking at her. Again, he asked: "Fresher?" She said: "Yes." He said, "Come with me." She wanted to resist, but then she wanted to see how it went. This was her first time being ragged by a guy!

She followed him as he walked towards Skylab. He walked five steps ahead of her. She had to almost run to keep pace with him. Something about his gait in the kurta reminded her of camels. She let the thought pass.

At Skylab, he asked her what she wanted to have. Demurely, she opted for a milk shake. He didn't order anything. She noticed Pappu (the kiosk owner) winking at this guy. They exchanged a few words in Rajasthani, including a 'Baad mein' (I'll pay later).

They went to a shaded area under a tree. He got out a pack of 'More' mentholated brown cigarettes from his kurta pocket and lit one. He pushed the pack towards her; she shook her head. This was going to be interesting.

He then proceeded to tell her about his life's ambition; to one day produce a movie which would be half in English and the other half in Hindi. It would be part South Indian and part North Indian. He had all the commercials and financials worked out.

She asked about the story. He said that wasn't an issue. It needed a North Indian Hero, and a South Indian Heroine, a vamp, a villain, a couple of fights, five songs, a rape scene, a couple of songs shot abroad, etc. By the time he had finished talking through his dream he had finished three of those long-stemmed cigarettes. She wished she could try one now, but he didn't offer again.

A bird in the tree above them was chirping: Chiru, Chiru, Chiru....

He then asked her whether she would like to act in the movie? This was now getting scary. She had visions of casting couches.

She then told him she had class. He offered to walk her back. She declined and ran....

X.

It was movie night!

She had a shower after lunch and got out her new jeans. Today was going to be special. It would be her first Hindi movie. Rajnikanth and Chiranjeevi: make way for Mr Khan!

She was going with some seniors; her excitement had been building up all day.

She heard them calling for her. With the last touch up of Ponds Dream flower talcum powder, getting the last curl in place with a drop of Parachute coconut oil, she set off following them.

They cycled gaily. Two of the girls were riding 'doubles'. She would never do that to her bike. She had a small nip of Old Monk before dinner, so there was an extra pep in her legs. The seniors thought she was just excited. They were so slow these girls; she hoped that they got good seats in the Audi.

As they passed Ram Bhawan, they had to slow down. Walking down the street, shoulder to shoulder were the 'Little Flower' boys. Dressed immaculately in bundgalas, sherwanis and polished shoes, exuding the tantalising scent of Hyderabadi 'ittar' (perfume).

Whilst the senior girls slowed down looking for space to pass; she rang her bell haughtily...after all Old Monk (not Red Bull) gives you wings!

With royal grace the guys quietly moved to the side, apologetically waving them on. After they had passed, she thought she heard words like: "Howla, chapplaan, mai ki *******;" etc.; she didn't care. They would be in time to get the best seats!

XI.

They parked near S Block. There was more space to park and easier to leave after the movie she was told. She carefully put the bike on the stand where the ground was level and followed the group.

The new jeans were stiff and uncomfortable. She should have stuck to her regular wear. As they neared the Audi, she bent to retie her shoelaces which had come loose. She got up with an audible 'sigh'.

There was a group of guys passing by. One of them smiled at her when she sighed; he thought she said "Sai!"

Leaning against the panelling next to the Audi door, was her saviour from the other morning, the guy who had fixed up her mud guard. He was standing with his legs crossed, weight on his right leg, wearing the same school uniform light blue shirt and jeans; only this time he was wearing chappals, with a red bandana round his neck, and a worn Stetson on his head. He was chewing on a sprig of hay.

Her heart started racing again. As she neared the Audi door, among the swarm of movie goers, he noticed her. His face broke into a shy smile. He tipped his hat. By this time she was blushing profusely. Her companions however were unaware and ushered her to their favourite seats. The moment had passed.

They settled down. Her companions were chattering away; she was blissfully in another place.

The lights dimmed. The movie was starting.

The latecomers were trying to find their friends in the dark. She saw a dark form in the aisle. Someone in the group of guys in front of them called out: "Allu!" The guy threaded his way towards the place where the call had come from. In another part of the Audi she heard someone call: "Sexy!" Three 'Saxenas' answered: "Aa raha hoon!" (Coming!)

... She wondered what sort of movie this was.

XII.

The movie meandered through the regular formula. The session with the kurta clad, camel-gaited guy in Skylab had made her lose her innocence with respect to movies. She kept mentally trying to tick the boxes: songs, one song in the rain, fight scene, rape scene, etc. The Khan was good but too chocolatey compared to her new hero; she wondered where he was. If only she had a couple of more swigs of the Old Monk, she would have followed the 'Sexys' with a 'Jat' or a 'Clint'...no one would know who it was in the dark...

During the interval, she told her companions she wanted to go to the toilet. She actually wanted to see whether she could see 'Clint' again.

He wasn't there, but a few stalls had cropped up in the foyer.

One said: Cheap home-made, Japanese formula 100-watt music systems; ready in 1 week; home delivery (room delivery to all hostels; gate delivery to MB).

The next one was: Fortune teller: we predict your CGPA! Free 'friendship' with 10 pointers on Facebook guaranteed for life.

The one after that had: Madraasi 'Alum': wholesale prices; order in any language, online preferable.

The movie was about to start.

XIII.

As she sauntered back into the Audi; a feminine voice called out from the balcony: "Sanjay!" followed by a raucous wolf-whistle.

There was sudden silence and then she saw about 50 or so guys stand up and look around.

What a sight!

Some were tall; some short; some clean-shaven; some moustachioed; some with designer beards; some fair; some dark; some smiling; some annoyed, some slim; some not so slim; some with lots of hair; some with receding hair lines; some unsure and shy; some confident ...

There was one thing common though: They all had a regal bearing, a grace in their movements as they rose from their seats and turned around, the haughtiness in their eyes from generations of royally evolved genes, the composure in their bearing...it seemed like she was in a swayamvar with 50 princes..

She could so easily picture them on magnificent steeds pounding the battlefields with valour and courage, princely turbans on their heads, long swords at their side.... Swoon!!!

XIV.

As the Sanjays settled down, she looked around and noticed that some of the 'couples' hadn't returned after the interval. Maybe they had found something more entertaining to do.

There was a noisy group in the first two rows banging chairs, calling for the movie to be started.

Out of the corner of her eye, she saw this guy staring at her. He looked like a good, intelligent boy. The curly hair that framed his small face had a sheen to rival her own. His checked, long-sleeved nylon shirt was iron pressed crisply, with a clean white singlet clearly visible underneath. His puny brown arms and chest showed lack of exercise; his eyes behind the black horn-rimmed glasses spoke of long hours of studying. He had sandalwood marks on his forehead.

The stare was disconcerting...it was expressionless, yet intense. Did she know him from her town or her coaching class? She looked away but couldn't help looking back. His gaze hadn't moved.

The lights dimmed and the movie commenced. Five minutes into the movie, there was a disco song on screen. The guys in the front seats were dancing. Too much Old Monk? Her shoulders gyrated slowly in sync with the beat. She was beginning to enjoy this. She stole a glance shyly towards the guy in the glasses. He was gone. His chair was empty.

XV.

It had been a long day. The dimmed lights, the last vestiges of Old Monk in her system, the raft of emotions she had been in the last few hours made her tired. She undid her laces, put her shoes under her seat, put her feet on the vacant chair in front of her, slid slightly forward and dozed off.

She dreamt...

She was in the town she grew up. The noise, the colour, the shops, the people. She thought of her dad. She loved him so much.

When she was small, every morning her dad would drop her off to school. She would sit behind him on his scooter, half asleep, holding on to him around his waist, her bag near his feet. As he weaved in and out of traffic, she couldn't see much; she just rested her face on his back.

She would come back home in an auto rickshaw with her schoolmates. After changing out of her uniform and a quick feed, she would go out to play in the street. At about 5.30 pm she would hear a beep. Her father was at the end of the street on his scooter. In the cacophony of beeps and horns, she could recognise his scooter beep. She would leave her friends and run to him. He would put her in the front of the scooter, and they would ride to their doorstep; she looking majestically at her friends and neighbours from her perch.

As her dad parked his scooter, she would take his lunch box and run to her mother.

Her mother would busy herself in the kitchen. Even though she didn't show it, she knew her mother was delighted, and this was the happiest part of her day. Whilst her father washed and changed, she would rattle to him all that she had learnt through the day.

One of his desires in life was to buy a car. This was a frequent topic of discussion in their house.

And the years went on.

She was in Class 12. Her dad would ferry her to tutorials and extra classes. Both her parents would pray for her success continually. The whole family was focussed on her doing well.

She couldn't forget how proud her dad was when she got her admission letter into BITS. He made photocopies and mailed it to all their relatives. He took the letter to show it to people at work. He was overjoyed.

Once they looked at the fee structure, she saw him slightly worried. However, he told her not to bother. He said the car could wait. The next few days that they spent in preparation for her to leave home and go to Pilani were a haze. Clothes, bedding, other stuff....

She remembered as she saw him off at Nutan as he boarded a bus to Delhi. He waved bye from the window. She knew his heart was breaking...

...Tears rolled down her eyes as she gently dozed in the Audi...

XVI.

Tall Dutta behind her got up and stretched. The creaking sounds from his joints woke her up. The movie was over, and the titles were running on screen. Tall Dutta was telling his companions 'loudly' about how mustard oil was better than coconut oil.

People were moving towards the aisle and out of the Audi. As they slowly trundled out, they reminded her of a mass of robots. People were trying to stay in their groups. A few were rubbing their eyes. She wasn't the only one to have dozed off.

She didn't remember much of the walk to their bicycles. She felt a coolness on her cheeks where the tears had dried.

Because of the slow-moving throng on the road past Ram and Budh, she couldn't ride; she had to wheel her bike.

Some of the guys swayed randomly as they walked. Her front wheel kept hitting some of them who strayed suddenly.

Something happened then which woke her up.

XVII.

One of the guys walking ahead of her called out "Srini!" From somewhere further down the road, someone answered back. The first guy shouted back: "Ball!" Then he started running as if to bowl. Magically the crowd parted for him, revealing a ready 'Srini' down the street. The imaginary ball was bowled; Srini batted it back with an imaginary bat, over the bowler's head. Someone shouted: "Catch it Ra!" Four guys converged to catch the imaginary ball descending from the trees. She ducked this way and that to avoid them.

She used the clearance in the road to mount her bike and ride away, narrowly missing the eager Srini, who was looking to see if he was caught! From behind her came guttural shouts of OUT!

As she went past the temple, some of the couples who had left during the interval were joining the crowd returning to MB.

XVIII.

She had now been in Pilani for two months. She felt like she had been here forever. The childish ragging had stopped as soon as tests had commenced. She had made a few friends including with some guys. Somehow, she found some of the friend circles were around the states or schools people came from...she went with it, but wanted to go out and explore...

She was picking up the lingo too...ghotu, lachaas, sidees, backies, etc.

This Saturday evening, she decided to skip the movie and have some quiet time by herself. Most people had gone to the movie except a 'ghotu' wingee who kept worrying about her CGPA...

She had been to C'Not earlier that day and picked up a bottle of Coke. Her favourite mess servant had delivered her dinner thaali to her room along with a jug of ice.

She changed into a pair of shorts she had bought to start jogging, dug up her Old Monk from her Safari suitcase, mixed a stiff drink, dragged her chair to the window, planted her feet onto the window sill, had a sip and started crooning to herself songs from her childhood.

She planned to buy one of those 100-watt systems from Bubba. For now she was satisfied with the gentle warm late evening desert breeze rustling through the neem trees outside her window, with the subdued cacophony of crows nesting for the night, an occasional tinkle of cycle bells of the locals who went past MB, the glorious aroma of Old Monk interspersed with the rising bubbles from the Coke, the clinking of ice, the condensation on the outside of the steel glass.

She remembered the famous last words of the Australian outlaw Ned Kelly: 'Such is Life'!

XIX.

She woke up next morning with a hangover. She has forgotten to put her thaali outside in the night and the smell of food was intense. She felt a dull pounding in her head. The pounding was rhythmic and was growing louder. She tried to sleep it off; but the beat continued, interspersed by the sound of running water.

She looked at her little alarm clock. It was 6:00 am and still dark outside her window. She got up and barefoot walked to the bogs in a daze. The pounding sounds had now stopped.

As she turned into the bogs, eyes half closed, she crashed into something...rather someone...... someone in a crisp purple nightie with white lace on the bodice wet near the feet, checked towel like a turban on her wet hair, one hand holding a bucket of washed clothes, the other holding blue Rin soap, a small bat (used to beat/wash clothes) under one armpit, smelling of Lifebuoy.

The crash resulted in the clothes falling out of the bucket, the bat falling on the nightie clad girl's toes, the Rin soap skidding across the floor. The towel on the head had unwrapped and covered this apparition's face.

She took advantage of the momentary blindness induced by the towel, and quietly slipped into the loo.

She could hear an angry burst in Bhojpuri, as the clothes and bat and soap and towel and bucket were being collected.

XX.

She took her time in the bogs after that encounter. Her heart was still thumping as she stood at the door of the bogs and looked into the corridor to see if everything was clear.

As she tiptoed to her room, she saw that Miss Bhojpuri's door was open. She was seated on the ground doing her puja, aggarbattis (incense sticks) in one hand. In the other hand was the bat steadily beating on a pair of ghungroos in sync with her gentle humming.

She moved on. At the other end of the wing, a tall girl from Coimbatore was practicing her model walk, with a Mod Phy and LinAl book balanced on her head.

She went on. The next door was open too. There was this girl from DPS in fluorescent green tights and hot pink top dancing to 'Born in the USA', hair dryer in one hand, a Gold Flake in the other!

She thought to herself: "This was too much!"

Just when she thought she had seen it all, she passed by another room, from which there were sighing sounds coming. Curiosity got the better of her. She peeped through the window.

There was this girl doing one arm push ups. Her walls were adorned with posters from Muscles magazine. She wore a white Rupa singlet, and with one arm behind her back. She was transfixed watching the flexing of her shoulder muscles and the triceps, well defined and tan in colour.

A drop of sweat started from her neck and made its way down her chest, gently soaking the white fabric of the Rupa singlet .... aahhh!

...she had her first girl crush!

XXI.

Last week in the Common Room she had watched the rerun of the Wimbledon Women's Final on Doordarshan.

It had been a gruelling match between Chris Evert and Martina Navratilova. As the match progressed, she oscillated between supporting the muscular Martina and the ladylike Chris. Her sidee kept a running commentary going on the rules of the game.

The tennis bug had bitten her...

She had seen a "For Sale" sign on the mess notice board selling, among other things a tennis racquet. She bought it.

Through the week, alone in her room, albeit without a ball, she practised her strokes... serves and volleys, two handed backhands, slices, top spin...the lot.

On Sunday afternoon, when the gym grounds were less busy, she ventured down to the courts in her white shorts, white keds, her racquet on her cycle carrier.

Cookie was there, in his Wimbledon whites, with his three balls, bouncing his serves off the gym wall. She parked her bike by the gym door.

Cookie flashed a fatherly smile at her, and she lost her shyness. She went towards him nonchalantly whirling her racquet. Cookie tossed her his lucky third ball.

She had her first serve against the gym wall. It bounced way off from where she expected.

After a few stray tosses, Cookie offered to assist her with her serve. He stood behind her, holding her arms. He asked her to hold the ball in the left hand, stuck to the face of the racquet in the right hand. On instruction, she tossed the ball into the sky, they both bent their backs in unison; he asked her to bend her knees and her right arm.

He guided her then to correctly unbend her right elbow and smash the ball into the wall. The ball bounced back and floated past them. Only then did he release her arms.

What a coach!

XXII.

It was the Diwali break. Most of the people from states close to Pilani: Delhi, Punjab, Rajasthan etc. had gone home. The campus felt different. There was a festive spirit in the air. Nutan and C'Not were full of locals and campus staff buying firecrackers and other stuff. The mithai shop and the tailors were especially busy. Attendance at the temple had gone up.

She had a lazy day that Sunday. She went in very late for lunch at the mess. Her favourite mess servant had saved her a bowl of hot pulao, mutter paneer, even a generous slab of Cassata ice cream. As she was the last one in the mess, she struck up a conversation with him. He was in his 40s, with a week's stubble on his chin, in his blue uniform. He had always been friendly and accommodating, with a ready smile; however, given the festive nature she asked him about his family.

She learnt he came from a village in Himachal as did most of his colleagues. He had studied until primary school, and then when his father died, started working in the fields to help his mother with family expenses.

He married when he was 18. His mother's failing health and losing their fields due to debt, forced him to look for other work. Another mess servant from his village brought him to Pilani. He went home every summer. In these 25 years he had 7 kids, of whom 5 had survived. His eldest son was working in the RPA mess. His wife and two of the kids now worked as domestic help in Shimla. Two of the smaller kids were with his wife's family.

She asked him whether he missed his family at Diwali. His smile dimmed. He turned his face away, and she saw him wiping away tears.

XXIII.

She was coming down from the S Block to the M Block for her Engineering Graphics class, her drafter on her shoulder. As she turned the corridor into M Block, she collided with some guy who was turning into S Block. He was obviously in a hurry.

This guy came off second best as her drafter poked into his soft and moderately ample mid-section. A few books and notebooks dropped to the ground and socialised with each other, as books do. As they both bent to sort and pick up their books, their heads collided, and his glasses fell over. It was like in the movies.

He smelt strongly of Brut cologne. She liked it! As she looked up, their eyes met. It was the guy from the tennis. He looked different in his crisp Kurta, well creased jeans, kolhapuri chappals and the gold rimmed glasses. She didn't mind the Brut, and took her time collecting her stuff.

He had said sorry about 10 times so far. With one hand he

massaged his hairy belly where the drafter had poked him. She looked at her drafter. It was slightly twisted from the impact.

As she tried straightening it, she felt a shadow behind her. A strong sinewy arm came over her shoulder, took the drafter from her hands. It was the guy who had repaired her cycle mudguard. With the same gentle smile, this Hercules from Haryana, in his blue short sleeved shirt and acid washed jeans, effortlessly twisted her drafter back into shape. He helped her collect her other stuff and doffed his imaginary Stetson. She could almost imagine a "Howdy Ma'am!"

Mr. Tennis 'Brut' walked off with Hercules after muttering his eleventh apology.

She continued to Engineering Graphics, her heart pounding.

XXIV.

She had her first puncture.

After a lazy Sunday morning, she had planned to replenish her Old Monk stock.

She would carry a little backpack to Nutan. Her favourite mess servant had introduced her to the Raju, the owner of the Student Refreshment Centre at Nutan.

She would park near his shop, order masala chai, (malai maar ke); give him her backpack and 80 bucks. By the time the tea arrived, he would deliver the Old Monk in the backpack. Very convenient.

Today, as she crossed the circle near Shankar, her rear tyre burst with a loud noise.

Cookie at the tennis courts was stretching for an overhead smash; the sound made him fall over flat on his ... The white shorts were now clay red on the behind.

Mallamal, enjoying his fourth bowl of steaming hot Maggi in the balcony outside Camel Gait's room in Bhagirath new wing upstairs dropped his spoon in shock. He went on eating using his fingers.

SRK in the Bhagirath bogs, broke his Pyjama nada (drawstring).

A Bihari wingee called to his sidee, saying that it sounded like a tinatta! (country made 303 pistol).

KV guy walking in a Wills navy cut haze, looked at the sky through his mop, looked at the canopy of trees, scratched his mop, and just walked on.

At Nagar's rehri, the guys eating hot gajar (carrot) halwa didn't even look up from their plates.

XXV.

The MB Open Freestyle Wrestling Competition had been announced.

There was a buzz in the corridors; in fact, all over the campus. She was excited!

There were to be 8 contestants. No fresher has ever contested. Feeling reckless after pushing her punctured bicycle, refreshed with a couple of shots of Old Monk; she threw her hat in the ring. There were plenty of (beautifully trimmed) raised eyebrows.

There were two contestants from Delhi competing, three from UP, one from Jaipur, one muscly one from Chennai, besides her.

The contestants were busy practicing. Each had chosen a 'stage' name. Very creative and scary ones. She had chosen a rather innocuous epithet: ' The Monk's Angel'.

There was a lot of posturing, especially when the contestants brushed past each other. One of the UPites would slap her thigh as a sign of aggression. Another would stare through thick mascara lined eyes. Yet another, left her hair loose, unbrushed with dreadlocks. The Jaipur one lifted her sleeve and flexed her biceps.

It was on!

XXVI.

The campus was resounding with drumbeats. Seemed like a clash of cultures, yet it was a crucible of joy, suppressed passion and unbridled desire to win.

The Delhiite's cheer squad had set up a Bhangra routine. GDBeds and co practised into the late hours. Balle! Balle! was the battle cry, interspersed with the Punjabi vocabulary delicacies of Behendi's and Maadi's! Chunnis were borrowed to make colourful turbans.

The Chennai girls had their own white dhoti clad topless 'band' based out of Ram-Budh-Malviya. Upper bodies painted as lions, elephants and bulls, they sashayed through the wings. They practised their eye, facial and finger expressions through the day!

The Jaipuri girl was behind schedule. Due to some misunderstanding, a shehnai band had come up in a tempo from Chirawa. They set up early in the morning outside MB. All the Sanjays wondered who was getting married.

The Balika Vidyapeeth girls complained as it was interfering with their school band drills.

She sent a mess servant to call in her own publicity manager Camel Gait! Wearing a red langot as a bandana, a long More menthol dangling from his lips, he arrived promptly. He nodded to the Chirawa shehnai crew as he waited for an audience.

She asked him about her own cheer squad. He said they were practising. She wanted to have a look. He took her to the Audi backstage. This time she led; he followed with his camel gait.

The music hit her before they got there. Electric guitars, keyboards, drums; bass, lead, bongos! The whole crew in red dyed Mohawks, tattoos with her name on their arms, chains, piercings, the lot. BioS saw her, turned around to the group...1,2,3,4... The room filled with the sound of the best anthem ever!

XXVII.

She parked her bike at the entrance of Ashok and strode purposefully to 118 in the front wing.

She knocked on the door. "Kaun hai?" (Who's it?) in earthy Haryanvi tones was the response. She didn't reply, just knocked louder. She heard a muffled "Behen di..., Maa di..." etc. as the bed inside creaked. The door opened. There was her dream coach, the guy who had muscled her bike mudguard and drafter into shape. He was wearing pyjama bottoms and nothing else. Gosh, he was so hairy!

For a moment she was speechless, but quickly recovered. One hand on the door frame, the other on her hip, she told him, she was recruiting him as her head coach! Before he had time to respond, she took out a spare red flag from her hip pocket and threw it on his bed. She stared deep into his eyes, daring him to decline.

Such was the power of her presence; he just nodded his acceptance. She smiled a little smile and pointed at his Pyjama top hanging on his chair. He quickly put it on. She beckoned him to sit on the balcony with her to discuss strategy and the rest of the team. They decided to recruit Cookie, the tennis pro, as psychologist; Jonty as the fitness coach; SRK as publicity manager and the would-be movie director as logistics manager. The rest of the crew would be recruited later.

The head coach's sidee Bubba got into it straight away. He had 5 hundred-watt systems waiting for delivery. He had them all going with songs of valour and courage. A cacophony, but unmissable for anyone passing Ashok Bhawan.

In the new wing Ashok, Tall Dutta stepped out from Room 112 in his loose cream singlet and checked towel showing his long Assamese legs. He bent his giraffe neck into the front wing to see what the commotion was about. He didn't have his glasses, so withdrew his neck, scratched himself and went back into 112.

XXVIII.

It was the day after the tournament. The campus was slowly waking up after the massive night. The matches had drawn record crowds at the improvised D Lawns venue. Stalls had been set up selling Coke, 'improved' Coke, popcorn, shikhanji, chai, chillums, etc.

There had also been stalls selling personally autographed contestant paraphernalia. The stalls played their respective anthems loudly. The Chief Warden is said to have monitored the event through his window and also occasionally sauntered to the fringes of the crowds, making eye contact with prospective troublemakers. The message, though unspoken, was clear.

Security reported the next day that the crowds were generally well behaved.

There were allegations and rumours aplenty of match-fixing, outside (local population) involvement, intimidation and the like; allegations that normally haunt such events. The Balika

Vidyapeeth band had played a few tunes to get the day going and had been there when the winner was crowned.

This morning, people had slept in late. Discussions about each match had gone late into the night in Nutan, C-Not and the wings. There were mixed emotions of disappointment, acceptance and plenty of backslapping in various languages interspersed with slang and other add-ons. An impromptu victory procession for the winner had taken off last night but was ceased very soon by the security guys.

The sweepers were busy cleaning the lawns, waking up some of the supporters who had spent the night in and around the D lawns. They had been unable to make the journey to their rooms. It looked like the whole campus had a hangover.

As for the participants themselves, they had an uneasy night because of the physical and emotional strains and bruises.

XXIX.

Her on-again off-again relationship with the Haryanvi coach continued. The wrestling tournament had meant that they spent a lot of time together. Whilst his physical and mental strength attracted her, his rigidity and casual attitude to life in general frustrated her.

They had a few arguments, where he had pushed back strongly when she tried to get to know him better.

She had convinced him to join the popular Zumba classes held in the Museum lawns led by the multi-talented swim Instructor. Thrice a week they participated in this high energy routine along with fifty others.

Today, it was quite humid and sultry. Clouds were building beyond the horizon over Malviya. She wished it would rain. She remembered the downpours in her hometown, how she would run into the street and splash around in the puddles. Her mother was usually very cross after that.

She wondered what her mother would think of this guy.

They sat exhausted after the class, resting against each other's backs, in silence. Nonchalantly, he plucked a blade of grass and chewed on it, staring blankly at the distant horizon. Sometimes, she wondered what his thoughts were, or was he just day dreaming. She rambled on about instructors, movies, mess food; he just continued in his blissful calmness, not responding, occasionally nodding.

SRK and Camel Gait passed by, arms around each other's shoulders, sharing a 'fag', with an exuberant: 'Kya haal hain, Jimmy?' (How are you, Jimmy?). By the time he replied with a slow drawl, "Theek…hai" …they had already disappeared over the next mound.

It was getting dark. It was funny how the cacophony of crows announced the advent of dusk, before the sun actually set. He rubbed his tummy, a sign that he was hungry. With an audible sigh, he asked: "Chalein?" (let's go?).

Without waiting for a response, he got up, slowly stretched his hands and back and started walking. She hurriedly picked herself, collected her stuff and followed.

She slowly slipped her arm into his as they walked. He continued to chew on the sprig of grass. They got to where she had parked her bike. She put her stuff on the bike carrier. He said 'Bye' and started walking to RBM mess.

She rode back to MB. It was getting dark.

XXX.

This was one of those mid-week lazy late afternoons. It was a non-religious Public Holiday. There was a break in the 'Tests' calendar. It looked like everything was in a state of inertia.

However, some people are not comfortable with inertia and want to move things, make things happen…silly!

Her coach loved inertia, and they lazed in a corner of C'Not, leisurely nursing their second cheeku shake, perfectly happy with each other's presence. Talk seemed to be not required.

They were now frequently seen together, so people didn't cast a second glance at them as a couple. The guys looked at her and looked away; she was 'taken'. She did not like it.

There was a group of guys sitting beside them in their own

circle, discussing random stuff. She picked up snatches of their conversation.

Bhalu and Moon had been for a ride to the gliding club this morning; Bhalu was seriously considering buying the gliding club and converting it into a farmhouse.

Moon's 20th birthday was coming up and he was looking for a venue to celebrate. He was also apparently receiving multiple cakes and gifts as parcels from prospective in-laws.

AJ kept an eye on the road for handsome and beautiful human models whom he could one day sculpt in marble.

GDBeds was polishing his photography skills, shooting random people. His long hair and luxurious moustache made him look very professional.

Jay heard all of them and 'straight-faced' freely proffered assistance with financial planning at discounted prices for these ventures.

XXXI.

It was 10.00 pm. They lay side by side in the Shiv Ganga lawns. They were spent.

Sweet smelling sweat still dripped from their faces into the grass. An ant made its way up her sleeve. She ignored it.

Their chests heaved in unison after the effort. The sensation of pleasure radiated from their bodies. She didn't want the feeling to end.

She extended an arm and gently raked her hand in the soft grass. She came up with a handful of dried neem leaves. Playfully she threw it at him. However, sapped of energy, it was a weak attempt and the leaves just fell back on her chest where they pulsated with her heaving and gently rolled back into the grass.

This was her first time. She had heard about it; sometimes on sleepless nights she had fantasised about it. Never did she realise it would be like this. The slow, unsure, fumbling start, whilst they explored. It was followed by deeper trust and acceptance. it became more natural and rhythmic; until it reached a crescendo where they both gave into the thrill and physicality of it all with random abandon.

And then, when it was over, they slowly crashed into the grass and lay where they were.

Words were unnecessary. Just silence...

Late night shadow boxing in SG lawns. She loved it!

XXXII.

She was in a pensive mood today. She had decided to bunk all classes and stay in her room. The past few weeks had been emotionally exhausting.

Her coach-cum-friend had made her lose her carefree, exuberant and spontaneous lifestyle. Last night, she had told him that she needed some space by herself, that they shouldn't see each other for a couple of weeks.

He had reacted typically. He just said OK and walked away nonchalantly in his slow, measured gait.

Spending so much time with him, she had neglected some of her friendships with the girls, besides writing home regularly. Her mum was always worried and wanted to know whether she was eating properly, how she was coping with the onset of winter; her dad wanted to know how her studies were going, whether the bike was working well, whether she had enough money. It was the same queries every week. They loved her and were anxious for her and she felt guilty about her annoyance with their questions. She had changed in the last few months; they didn't know.

Even the schedule of classes, tests, make-ups, etc. was becoming routine. There were no surprises in the mess food either.

She lay on her bed and stared at the squeaky, cream coloured ceiling fan slowly rotating, circulating the warm mid-morning air. The regulator was busted, and she could either have it at 1 or 5. She needed to get it fixed. Chiranjeevi and Rajnikanth on the wall looked more like make believe plastic characters rather than real people.

She got up, turned the fan regulator to 5, lay down again, pulled the blanket over her head and went to sleep.

XXXIII.

There was a buzz in the campus about the cricket world cup. It looked like everyone was playing cricket. There was a game on in almost every wing. Used tennis balls were in high demand. Cookie hid his three balls and gave up tennis for three weeks. His time was now spent on doing critical reviews of all the umpires, especially the English ones. Camel Gait had fashioned his own bat using a combination of old Debonair and Manohar Kahaniyaan magazines. He thought the centrefold would distract the bowlers. He soon found out that it was distracting the wicketkeeper more.

The attire was a random mix of lungis, dhotis, pyjamas, shorts, etc. The only wing where the attire was traditional English whites was the 'Little Flower' Hyderabadi Nawab wing. Even their appeals were laced with Nawabi Tehzeeb, unlike the raucous cacophony of the other wings.

The MBites felt a bit neglected. There were fewer 'guests' at the gates. The main social haunts wore a deserted look.

As she sat on the S Block steps; the cricket fever was in evidence even in the usually sacred Insti corridors. Pras walking from the library, respectfully asked her if she could look after his books for ten minutes. She agreed. He then stood there, limbered up and ran down the corridor in his bell bottoms and chappals practising his 30-yard run up to bowl a Jeff Thomson type delivery. He has been working on his hair too. He bowled a mock 'over' and then collected his books from her and walked back to his Bhawan.

KV guy was returning from Skylab on his way to IPC. He had fashioned a couple of balls by squishing a few packets of Wills Navy Cut. He was now tossing his balls in the air at different angles and different heights and trying to catch them in mid-flight. Every successful catch was marked with a 'What Eh!'. One of his balls fell in her lap, she threw it back at him. It was a bit greasy and smelt. She plucked a leaf from the bush near her and wiped her fingers.

She noticed bespectacled Anime sitting at the other end of the steps, wearing his trademark sky-blue jacket. He had a notepad and a calculator in his hand. He looked at her, winked and whispered. He was offering 2:1 odds on the India-Pak match on the weekend. She politely declined.

She heard a loud "OUT!" from inside the S Block corridor. Was someone playing cricket in there, she wondered. DD emerged from the Chief Warden's office. The Chief Warden repeated after him "Out!"

Jay walked down with a yellow shirt and a bandana round his head. His shirt was unbuttoned exposing his hairy chest. He wiped his brow on his wrist band; muttering "Lillie! Lillie!! Lillie!!!"

XXXIV.

It was Valentine's Day. There was passion and excitement in the air!

This year the MMS guys had taken up a project of setting up a small fair on the pavement leading to MB as a project. Advance marketing had gone on through various channels to maximise demand for the products on offer. Plenty of research had gone into product development and placement. For the past few weeks, the MMS guys had done customer surveys assessing customer sentiment and market trends. The local competition (Nutan, Skylab and C'Not) had been kept in mind. Finally, they decided on three main stalls.

There was the mandatory Archie's card and flower stall to start with. This stall also had inflatables (balloons, swimming pools for two, etc.).

The next one was a stall offering piercings and tattoos. Both permanent and temporary tattoos were available and a tattoo artist from Begum Bazaar, Hyderabad had been brought in.

After that came the bottle shop, with miniature wine and champagne bottles with pink bows sold with complimentary miniature ice buckets.

There was music. Elvis, Sinatra, Pankaj Udhas and Kishore took turns in setting up the mood.

XXXV.

It was the 'March of the 10 pointers' Day!

This Monday was declared a holiday, a day intended to celebrate the most brilliant the campus had. It was her first one and by the talk and the anticipation that had been building up across campus, she knew it was going to be big.

The march commenced at the Post Office went past RP Bhawan and the workshop, wound its way in front of C Block and M Block. The Diro and senior Insti faculty were seated on a podium at the Audi steps to acknowledge these great minds. The march then went past S block and concluded at Sky.

She woke up early to get a good vantage point along the route. Some people had camped overnight along the road. Banners with their favourites, were strung on the hedges lining the route.

It started 25 years ago as a way to acknowledge the 10 pointers and slowly by public demand, now included everyone over 9.314 CGPA.

There were 40 of them marching this year; 30 belonging to year 1 and 2.

At the start of the march they were mounted on to rickshaws, a plaque near the handle-bar bearing their name and CGPA. A mess servant walked behind the rickshaw with a large umbrella to shield their delicate skin from the sun.

The Balika Band played: Hum hongey kaamyaab ek din! (We will be successful one day!)

There was a roar at the RP end as the march began. Necks strained to catch a glimpse of these magnificent men and women; the finest of the human race. The bystanders watched with awe and humbly clapped. The '10 pointers' nodded at the crowds and acknowledged their appreciation. As each rickshaw passed the Audi podium, the Diro and the entire faculty stood up and clapped.

Every 500 meters on the way, rehri's (street food carts) were placed for the rickshaw riders, to keep them hydrated. Nagarji had a special menu for each one according to their dietary needs.

As the last rickshaw passed, she wondered where these men and women would be 25 years from now; what magnificent change they would bring to people's lives and this world. She would be able to tell her grandchildren one day that she had witnessed greatness!

Her own hydration mix (Coke and Old Monk) bottle was nearly over. Time to head back to her room...

XXXVI.

She stared at the slow-rotating ceiling fan above her head as she lay on her hospital bed. She had just woken from an afternoon nap, when the nurse had come to change her IV bottle. She felt weak. Tomorrow morning, she would go back to MB.

It happened when she was cycling back to MB, after the March of the 10 pointers. She suddenly felt the world going dark. She managed to get off her bike and sit on the kerb. She didn't remember much after that but woke up at the Sarvajanik hospital. The doctors said it was dehydration and sun stroke. The Old Monk wouldn't have helped much.

She had some visitors off and on. The wrestling competition participants had all come together. Instead of flowers they all wore 'red' headbands...her colour! They stood around her bed in silence. Their eyes communicated their respect for a fellow wrestler. They were uneasy seeing her lying on the bed, pale and weak. Finally, the Jaipuri wrestler tapped the UP wrestler on her tush (as wrestlers do) - a signal...time to go!

In contrast to these muscular specimens were the skinny Malayalee nurses buzzing around.

Her coach hadn't been in, she doubted he knew about her being in hospital. In a way, she was relieved; he wouldn't know how to cope with it.

Every time she slept, she had nightmares. This guy, one of the '10 pointers' kept coming up in her dreams. The dream changed every time, but it was always him. She remembered, then. She was having a swig from her coke bottle when his rickshaw had passed during the march. He had looked at her with a distaste, as if thinking "How dare she drink instead of staring at me in awe."

The night before she had dreamt of him being her boss. Last night, he was her husband. It was so bad, that she screamed and jumped out of bed. The IV lines pulled her back. The night nurse came scurrying and enquired what was wrong. Dazed, she asked her to get the guy out of her bed!

The night nurse was nice. Shakila even had a beau! A Tom Brady look-alike; he visited her every night...

XXXVII.

The call came rather late and threw her in a quandary.

There had been rumblings for a number of years in Meera Bhawan about removing the 11.00pm-7:00 am curfew.

There was a call now to launch an agitation and her name had popped up to lead it. She was stunned. She felt excited that she had been considered as a leader; or maybe, just the fall person.

The merchant associations of Shiv Ganga Market (aka C'Not) and Nutan Market had offered to fund the agitation, anticipating a growth in business. The IMFL shop had promised her a year's supply of Old Monk, delivered to MB (suitably camouflaged).

It was interesting.

She convened a meeting of her wrestling support crew; no MBites at this one. Jimmy, Camel Gait, Cookie, Jonty and she met at a secret undisclosed location at Nihali Chowk one Sunday afternoon. The boys were all in mufti; white, slightly soiled, kurta pyjamas to blend with the locals. She herself wore a salwar suit and decided to forgo the coconut oil this once.

As they sat on the charpoys; Camel Gait passed the hookah around. Jimmy said it reminded him of a khap panchayat. Cookie took minutes; whilst Jonty stretched his hamstrings against the charpoy strings. Tea was served in kullads (clay cups).

After long, slow deliberations, her team suggested that she accept the leadership of the agitation.

The campaign was ready to be launched. Messages of support were pouring in from Alumni, including some ex MBites who had suffered the lifelong emotional and psychological scars of living behind 20-foot walls and night curfews for 4 years.

XXXVIII.

It was a sunny, autumn Sunday afternoon. A few stringy clouds floated high in the blue grey sky. The sun was bright but not hot; just warm enough not to offend. The gentle breeze blew in short wafts, almost lazily, ruffling the tree leaves, and then giving up.

She decided it was a great day for fishing.

She found fishing on the banks of SG stream therapeutic. It was lonely there in the afternoons, beautiful green lawns; clear, slow-moving stream of water; well behaved trout.

She got her gear ready. Fishing rod, low calibre twine, hooks, flies. She decided to use live bait, plenty of worms behind the mess.

She rubbed on some sunscreen lotion and got into her fishing gear. Khaki cargo pants, sky blue sleeveless muscle top (her coach's gift), knee length boots and a wide brimmed straw hat with pink lace.

She also packed up her icebox with some ice from the mess with a couple of Hayward's 5000's tossed in. The ice box would come in handy to keep the fish she caught as well. She packed up a packet of Now and a lighter in one of the pockets of the cargo pants, the pudiya of green tobacco in the other.

She put up a punch card on her door. It said: 'Gone Fishing'.

She packed all her stuff on her bike and walked it to the stream. Finding a shady spot, she unloaded her gear, leaned the bike against the bushes, laid out her folding-chair. Carefully, she put a worm on the hook and cast her first line.

She knew from experience, that the first fish was the hardest to catch. Fishing taught one patience.

She settled down in her chair to wait, watching the float shimmer in the autumn sun. Below the surface, she could see small bubbles forming. There were fish there. One would bite soon.

She fixed up a Now cigarette and lit up. Next, she drew out an ice-cold beer, uncorked it with her teeth, spat out the lid and had a long swig. She rested her feet on the ice box. A puff, a swig, another puff, another swig...

She felt happy with the world. Fishing was therapeutic...

XXXIX.

The Didi club was in session. She had been 'invited'!

A bonfire had been lit in the quadrangle. Ten moodas had been placed in a circle around the fire for the club elders. Five moodas without backrests had been placed in an outer circle for the privileged invitees.

The babool tree branches had been lit earlier in the evening by the chosen mess servant. Besides him, no other mess servant was allowed in. He was sworn to secrecy.

The 10 Didis marched in a column. It was slow gentle march. They all wore black salwars and red shawls as part of the occasion. The shawls covered their heads. They walked with a slow measured gait, conscious of their high calling as members of this elite club.

The club was an enigma by itself. It wasn't a recognised body. There were no elections; new members were nominated by members who passed out. There were unwritten rules on the nominations, never publicly disputed.

They met monthly. The invitees were prospective members. They wore white salwars and black shawls.

As the babool branches crackled in the winter air, blowing sparks into the clear night sky, the Didis marched in. The invitees bowed low; hand crossed across their chests. The Didis took their seats. It being a cold night, they all wore black woollen socks.

They settled down in their moodas, gently groaning in recognition of the softness and the comfort of the moodas. The mess servant passed around steel glasses and then poured in hot, steaming masala chai, spiced with secret herbs into the glasses. The guests were served tea from another jug, minus the secret herbs. She didn't mind. She felt privileged to be here. Moreover, she had her 'Coke' bottle with her, hidden in her shawl.

This was a slow measured meeting; there was no rush.

As the chai and the heat from the bonfire made the Didis' cheeks go red; one of them stirred as if from a trance and mumbled a few words to the group. The rest nodded.

A drafter was passed around. The one who held the drafter had the floor. The mess servant passed it around. He wore gloves.

They then discussed various topics of interest concerning MB and the Insti in general. Decisions were taken over a few more cups of spiced masala chai. As they spoke, the steam from the chai mingled with the smoke from the fire and their own foggy breaths and rose into the firmament. The invitees watched in awe.

As the night grew dark, and the embers died down, the drafter was put back into its sheath. One by one the Didis got up, stretched to get the circulation back into their muscles, emptied the last dregs of tea from their glasses into the fire. The fire hissed spitefully. The Didis walked back to their rooms.

The invitees hung around for some time, reverently looking at the empty moodas and slowly dispersed. The mess servant cleaned up after them.

The full moon had sunk below the horizon...

XL.

The MB music night was coming up.

Hosted inside MB, it was to be a 24-hour event. It had commenced a few years ago as a way to getting back at the Balika Band's annoying drums.

There were groups, soloists and duets.

As happened every year, in the beginning of the year groups were formed, some fell out during practice and re-formed with different combinations. Some ended as soloists, others got matched with whoever would accept them. Wingee broke up with wingee, and the competition generated a general air of... well... competition!

She couldn't sing. So, she assigned herself to the stage management and production team.

Four weeks before the event live stage rehearsals commenced. Newcomers tripped over wires; Swearing in Tamil. Telegu, Punjabi, Haryanvi, Marwari, Cat English, Bhojpuri, Malayalam and the soft tones of Bengali were heard.

The backstage area was of immense importance. Besides having change and makeup rooms and logistic support groups, there was the 'little' *(in size)* girl who sat on a wooden crate in a dimly lit corner. The crate was padlocked with three different locks. She sat on it with an expressionless face, leaving only for toilet or meal breaks. Rumour had it that she even slept on the crate. For those in the know, the crate contained the liquid and herbal nutrition required to sing well, let one's hair down and forget one's inhibitions...

The mosh pit area was laid with a new layer of river sand. The security girls, dressed like ninjas were placed on either side of the stage with lathis and cattle prods.

The team going so far, were the Mumbai Chats! They had adopted Pink as their model. Props included bicycles without mudguards, sharpened drafters, and psychedelic lighting accentuated by the fluorescent pink tube tops and Kylie Minogue leather shorts.

Then came the Bhojpuri team which had Ila Arun as their coach. They had tied their chunnis around their waists, with nunchakus tucked in. They swung the nunchakus around between verses. They painted their faces charcoal black with pink rouge. The only accompaniment to their songs was a dhol carried by a well-built 6-foot-tall drummer.

The Bengali group was the sweetest. White cotton sarees with silk borders, chubby brown cheeks, curly hair permed with mustard oil, they crooned sweet melodies, which they made up as they sang. They always smiled. Their leader kept sweetly smiling too, and after every song softly crooned Bhalo! Ati Bhalo!! and handed out KC Das rossogulas which further swelled the chubby cheeks.

XLI.

It happened one Friday evening...

It had been a normal boring week: tests, classes, mess, dhobi, postie, shikhanjis at Skylab, shopping rides to C'Not, gossip in the wings...

She was returning from Nutan. As she cycled slowly past the gate and swimming pool, she thought she saw her ex-coach/ friend/ lover riding from the Ashok main gate towards C'Not. Their eyes met even at that distance and they slowed down. They stopped at the corner of Ashok next to each other. She smiled shyly; it had been sometime since they had met or spoken. He stared at her with that same annoying half smile; still not speaking. He still wore his light blue half sleeved shirt and acid wash jeans. The stubble on his chin was a few days old.

She tried to stare back at him, to hold his gaze; but as usual, it didn't last long. Her eyes dipped to his broad chest.

She was uncomfortable but didn't want the moment to end.

In the background, his sidee in the Ashok front wing, Bubba, turned up the volume on Mariah Carey's "I can't live without you."

The atmosphere was emotionally charged. The coach reached out to hold her hand and with a quiet nod asked: "C'Not?" She nodded softly: "Yes."

Hand in hand they walked to C'Not; their other hands wheeling their cycles.

Rickshaws rode past, tinkling their bells; birds chatted animatedly in the trees above; soft music wafted from some of the Instructors' houses on the left; shouts of 'Howzzat' came from the cricket nets on the right...

They walked oblivious to it all. Remembering all the times they had spent together their grip on each other's hands tightened, the gap between them narrowed, as the two walked as one.

XLII.

They walked towards C'Not in silence.

They walked close to the edge of the pavement. Some people passing by gave them quick, meaningful glances. A group returning to RP passed commented under their breath. They didn't care.

She wanted to say a hundred things; it had been so long. She didn't want to ruin the moment though, so she kept quiet. Holding hands, their palms communicated their feelings and how much they had missed each other.

They heard anguished cheeping from a bush as they walked past. They ignored it at first; then he stopped to look back. Slowly he let go off her hand, put his cycle on its stand and went to see where the sound was coming from. She stood where she was and watched.

He bent down and slowly reached under the bushes. There was a sparrow in his hand, which fluttered briefly in fright and then weakly quietened down. One of its wings was broken. It had also lost some its feathers; it looked like it had been attacked.

There was a puddle of water on the roadside. He reached into the pocket of his jeans, removed a handkerchief, dipped it in the puddle and squeezed some drops of water on the bird's beak. The sparrow opened its mouth and drank. After a few more drops over the next few minutes, its eyes showed stronger signs of life. He placed it on the ground. The sparrow tried to hobble away but collapsed.

In the meantime, a group of school kids had gathered around him to see what he was doing. One of the kids opened her lunch box and offered a small piece of bread. He made minuscule pieces of the bread and placed them in his palm. The bird slowly pecked and ate a few pieces. He squeezed some more water from his handkerchief. He was now on his haunches, very much at home, just as he would have been in his village. She leaned on her bike, watching awestruck.

He turned around and asked her if she wanted to keep the sparrow as a pet. She was queasy. They sat on the pavement for the next hour as they bird rested between them.

It was getting dark. She decided to take the bird back to her room in MB. In the front cane woven basket on her cycle, they carefully arranged her chunni. They put a few pieces of bread as well. They put the bird in there, covered with a bit of the chunni, and closed the basket lid.

She waved bye and cycled slowly to MB. The bird slept peacefully.

He squeezed the last drops from his handkerchief, tied it around his neck, put his Stetson back on, wheeled his bike around, and rode back to Ashok. The sun set behind him.

XLIII.

She rode slowly to MB, conscious of the bird with the broken wing in her basket.

As she rounded the Vyas bend, she saw Kant walking down

the pavement with a calculator in his hand. He did IT returns consultancy for the staff as a side business. Watching her ride so delicately, he raised his palm in a questioning manner.

She didn't want to stop or take her hand off the handles. So, she just lifted her middle right finger off the handle.

Kant being a person of high IQ caught on immediately.

He raised his arms and fluttered it like wings. She nodded and put her finger back around the handle.

He gave her a thumbs up and returned his gaze to the calculator.

XLIV.

She woke up tired the next day. It had been a long night. Her lights had been on until 3:00 am, when she remembered throwing a pillow at the switch, to put it off.

She had arrived the last evening with the bird in her basket. As she climbed the stairs to her room, the bird had woken up and begun cheeping. A group of wingees going to the mess noticed and went back with her to her room. The windows were closed, and they peeped at the bird. It was fluttering around, looking at the mass of faces looking at it.

Her quick thinking sidee went in search of a girl whose dad was a vet. She came in, and immediately took charge of the situation.

A couple of girls were dispatched to fetch some neem twigs. Another was sent to borrow some knitting wool from one of the Bengali girls.

The twigs of neem arrived. The 'vet' girl removed a Rambo knife from the folds of her Rajasthani ghaghra and whittled a couple of splints from the neem branches.

The Bengali girl was about to call it a night when someone came knocking for wool.

She decided to check for herself what the wool was being used for and soon arrived at the door and gently knocked.

They made way for her as she wafted in, in her Victoria's Secret chiffon nightwear, with a basket of choice of wool on her elbow.

The 'vet' girl smirked in disgust at all this finery and snatched the nearest ball of wool. She then had the bird held by one of the super senior girls (who was in some sort of daze) and proceeded to expertly apply the splints to the wings.

She also ground some paracetamol into powder and put a little of it in a spoon of water and gave it to the thirsty bird.

She then swished off, the Rambo knife disappearing into the folds of her ghagra.

The Bengali girl tried to sing the bird a lullaby, however the excitement of it all was terrorising the bird. It was evident by the increasing bird droppings in the chunni in the basket.

They all left leaving her alone with the bird. Someone had her food delivered to her room from the mess. She ate hungrily.

She lay on her bed thinking of her reunion with the coach that afternoon. However, every so often the bird in the basket would commence cheeping again disturbing her thoughts.

Finally, she removed her Old Monk bottle from under her bed and sprinkled a few drops on the walls of the basket. The bird didn't cheep much after that.

It was 3:00 am. She threw her pillow at the light switch and dozed off.

XLV.

Next morning...

The MB mess secretary had donated some rice and wheat grains as bird seed to feed the sparrow.

There were a couple of grains fallen on the ground near the basket. She picked them up and looked at them.

They were wheat grains. They looked different though. The shape, serrations, colour and smoothness of the two grains were out of the ordinary. It puzzled her. As she looked at them more intensely, her anxiety increased. She put the two seeds in her kerchief, tucked the kerchief in her right shirt pocket and rode to Vyas Bhawan, where her BioSciences ghotu friend lived.

Standing at the main entrance, she called out his nickname.

It was 7.00 am. After 10 minutes of calling, the chowkidar

came out to see her. She showed him the seeds. The chowki went up to the back wing, upstairs and knocked at a door.

A voice from inside asked: "Kaun hai?" (Who's it?)

The Chowki replied loudly: "Sahib, aapke liye ek ladki aayee hai." (Sir, there's a girl for you downstairs).

Quite a few doors opened in the wing.

She had been waiting for about 10 minutes. A few guys were peeping from their windows at her surreptitiously. 218 had already been to the bogs, but he changed into a crisp new kurta pyjama and made an unscheduled walk to the bogs anyway.

119 wanted to go to the mess for breakfast. He took the long route. He walked all the way to the centre of the hostel, and then made his way to the back wing enroute the mess.

222 opened his door, peeped out, went back in, dabbed on another layer of Ponds Dream flower talc, tried to hide his acne and then walked down the stairs.

217 was sitting on the balcony upstairs in his lined pyjamas and janghiya chewing on a neem twig (brushing his teeth). With his left hand, he casually flipped through his Linear Algebra notes.

125 had finished breakfast. He had an Engineering Graphics class at 8:00 am. Usually he would walk through the back wing of Vyas to 168 Shankar, where his classmate and friend of 18 years from school joined him. They would walk to M Block together.

Today, he polished his shoes and his drafter holster, checked the crease on his bell bottoms, adjusted the oily, luxurious, curly lock on his forehead and purposefully marched through the front gate of Vyas, marched past her.

She watched, she waited....

The sun was now filtering through the tree leaves on her. She reached into the left front pocket of her shirt and removed a plastic flat cylinder. The cylinder had two compartments and a cap at either end.

One compartment had tobacco, the other lime (chuna). She took a portion of each and mixed them on her left palm, pressing down with her right thumb. She slapped the mixture a few times to remove the flaky bits and then pinched the remainder and deposited it in the back of mouth under the tongue. She wiped her palms on the back of her jean shorts.

She waited...

The Shankar Bhawan Warden had stepped out in his lungi for his early morning smoke. He saw her waiting by the Vyas gate and sauntered over.

She didn't recognise him and met his stare. He enquired what she was doing there. She spat out tobacco juice into the bushes and said she was waiting for the BioSciences friend. When he asked why, she took out the two seeds from her front right shirt pocket and showed them to him. He looked at them puzzled.

She asked him whether he could spare a smoke. He gave her one and lit the cigarette for her. They both looked at the Vyas main stairs, waiting for the friend to descend. A general hush was going through Vyas: the warden was at the gate.

She asked the warden whether he was the chowki of Shankar, as he had sauntered from that direction. He said he was the warden. She said "Sorry."

They smoked in silence for five minutes. The warden stubbed his cigarette and walked back to his house. He had a class at 9:00 am. She thanked him for the cigarette.

She waited...

There was a sudden hushed silence in all of Vyas. A door in the upstairs back wing had opened and closed. All eyes were riveted towards the main stairs.

Even the birds went silent. She noticed the change in energy and looked up at the stairs. From her vantage point, she could see only the lower half of the stairs before they turned and went up.

She held her breath. Feet clad in Cambridge green socks and Kolhapuris made their appearance first, followed by the tall, long haired gentleman in his simple but meticulously clean white kurta pyjama.

Adding to his aura, was his acolyte, named Sanjay, who followed behind him respectfully. He held his portable lab case.

No words were necessary. He made his way towards her, expressionless. She quietly removed the two seeds from the kerchief in her right front pocket, careful not to drop them.

He took both seeds in a gloved hand and looked at them through his monocle.

In the meantime, 'Lab kit' Sanjay had opened his case awaiting the expert's requests.

The Prof asked for three test tubes; one as a benchmark, the other two with soils samples of different alkalinities. The two seeds were placed in the two tubes, whilst the benchmark test tube received a normal wheat grain.

'Lab kit' Sanjay gave her a receipt with a reference. She could track the progress of investigations online. She mounted her bike and rode back to MB.

The bird in her room would be wake.

XLVI.

She had a visitor that evening.

The sun had set. It was 8:00 pm. He was announced as 'M'. She didn't know any 'M' and didn't want to leave her bird alone. However, being a fan of Bond movies; the 'M' intrigued her, and she decided to check him out.

She found this debonair gentleman at the gate. He was dressed in a crisp silk Lucknavi chikan kurta pyjama and qawwali singer's cap.

He bowed and greeted her, one hand behind his back. Then he extended the hand from behind him and presented her with a long-stemmed red rose.

She blushed profusely. She was overtaken by his charm and suddenly felt under dressed, under made-up.

He asked if they could move to a side and have a quick chat. She followed him dazed. He introduced himself as the sachiv (secretary) of the Hindi Drama Club (HDC). He had observed her this morning in front of Vyas and felt she would be the ideal leading lady for the upcoming HDC production: the Hindi version of Waiting for Godot.

She didn't know what to say, having never acted in a play before!

He spoke quietly, convincing her that she was the ideal person for the role. She gave in. She said she would give it a try.

He produced a document, asking her to sign. The main clause was that she was restricted from talking to the English Drama Club or to any of their talent scouts.

She signed. He pocketed the contract.

It was time to leave. He bowed again. She turned and ran up to her room, very excited.

XLVII.

Mainpuri was 'the' gentleman of the 83 second semester batch. Quiet, calm, affable; he was the epitome of respect and dignity.

Mainpuri conducted his affairs of the earthly world and the supernatural world from 109, Ashok Bhawan.

He didn't have the best of sidees. Whilst 108 spent his time either in the gym or sleeping or in the mess or having Old Monk fuelled 'events'; 110 was an '84 batch guy, who treated Mainpuri as a dad. He was petulant, demanding and constantly seeking attention.

Saturday afternoons between 13:38 and 14:47 hours, Mainpuri would do a special social service. This was really appreciated by people around the campus struggling with tests, CGPA, ACB, Warden's attention, lack of funds, strange dreams and quite often love.

Mainpuri was an established palm reader.

At 13:00 hours on Saturdays, 109 and 110 would wash the veranda between 108 and 110. They would then pull out the wooden bed from 109 and cover it with a white sheet.

Mainpuri would then have a cold-water shower singing bhajans loudly *(louder in winter for obvious reasons)* and come out dressed in white traditional Eastern UP garb. 110 would arrange a couple of pillows for Mainpuri to sit on.

At about 13:30 hours, a queue would start forming. 110 would ensure the queue was orderly and there were no priorities given to anyone ...even if they were from UP or were wingees.

All this while, a slight snoring sound would be emanating from 108. A sinister looking 'Sleeping. Do not Disturb' sign written on a punch card was posted in the window.

Today, however, there was a change in the normal order of things.

110 saw from the corner of his eye, an MBite stopping on the road. He wondered.

She put her bike on the stand, took the basket off the front handle and joined the queue.

Up until this time all the clients had been male. 110 started processing this new challenge.

Full of typical Benarasi chivalry, he went up to her with folded hands and asked her to come to the top of the queue. Someone protested. 110 replied: "Ladies queue." The protest died down quickly.

Mainpuri was advising a lovelorn KV guy who was missing his school sweetheart in T Nagar, Chennai.

She observed the proceedings with quiet wonder and awaited her turn with growing anticipation.

KV guy was done. He touched Mainpuri's feet respectfully and left. Mainpuri signalled to the next guy in the queue; however, 110 stepped in and whispered in his ear: "Guruji, there is an MBite who wants to see you."

Unruffled, Mainpuri asked her to come forward. She touched his feet as she had seen KV guy doing. He asked her to extend her palm. She said that she didn't want her palm read.

She then reached into her basket and proffered the bird with the broken wing.

Placing the bird in his lap, she gently asked: "Guruji, when will my bird be able to fly?"

XLVIII.

The Medical Centre on campus was open.

Monday mornings were busy. Quite a few people were 'sick' because of excesses on the weekends. They were looking for medical certificates to get make-ups for scheduled tests. On Sunday evenings, the generous old doctor used to sit by the fire at home and fill up medical certificates. As people arrived on Monday, all he needed to do was to fill in names. Real military efficiency!

This Monday, it was cold and drizzly. As the doctor walked

into the medical centre, he noticed an unusual couple in the waiting room. They looked like students; at the same time, they also looked like doting parents. The man was in a light blue short sleeved shirt and acid washed jeans, with a blue muffler around his head. He had a two-day stubble on his steely chin. She was dressed in a white salwar kurta and covered with a shawl. She was holding what looked like a baby inside the shawl. Both 'parents' looked very concerned and were 'coochie-cooing' the baby.

The other people waiting were quite enamoured of this domestic scene.

The doctor settled down in his room, had a sip from the army flask he had brought from home and asked the nurse to send the couple in.

They came in; she gingerly holding the 'baby' under her shawl. He followed, holding her purse and bicycle keys.

She sat across the doctor and looked up worried. He said: "Beta, can I see your baby?" She exchanged a quick glance with her coach standing behind her. He gently laid his hand on her shoulder to reassure her. She unwrapped her shawl to reveal the basket with the bird.

The doctor's eyes widened as he looked into the eyes of the sparrow.

He had dealt with many an excuse for make ups in his time. This was most unusual!

XLVIX.

30 years on...

It was Valentine's Day. She was having a candle lit dinner with her husband of 25 years. It was their wedding anniversary as well.

It was a beautiful restaurant, high in the mountains. A fire crackled in the background. Outside, she could see the lights in the village at the bottom of the valley. Snowflakes fell gently and settled on the pine trees.

There was a violinist playing haunting melodies in the corner. The Pinot was refreshing.

For the hundredth time, she touched the sparkling diamond ring he had surprised her with that morning.

They didn't talk much. It was good to be silent. Occasionally, they locked eyes over the glow of the candle in the centre of the table. His eyes, as always, were pure. He hadn't stopped doting on her, even though it was now 25 years. She blushed. The warmth of the fire and the Pinot made a perfect romantic atmosphere.

As always, he was impeccably attired. They had shopped in Paris before coming here. She loved her ruby red gown. They had made quite an entrance into the restaurant.

As the music captivated her, she closed her eyes and thought about the years gone by. She had lost contact with most of her friends from BITS. Only recently, through social media, she had connected with a few. However, after the initial euphoria of meeting reconnecting with someone after a number of years, they had got caught up in their jobs, careers, families. It wasn't the same anymore.

He had been planning this holiday in the Swiss Alps for a few months. He had had a successful career heading his own software company. Their two sons were in Universities overseas. She had had a corporate career for a few years after graduating, but the demands of the kids and the challenges of finding a job in the same place as her husband made her shrink her career into an on-again, off-again consultancy.

Once the kids had left home, she worked with some NGOs. Life was pleasant.

He excused himself to go to the toilet. She looked around. There were three other couples dining, two older than them.

In a corner by himself, was a man dining alone, staring out of the window. It was dark in that corner. He wore a Swiss hat and a red scarf over a sky-blue shirt. As the glow of the fire played on his rough jaw line and wide shoulders, something felt familiar. She turned away. She didn't want to be caught staring.

The maître' D' came over to her table and placed a glass of what looked like lime juice (it had ice, a few lime seeds some pepper flakes floating). He bowed and whispered: "Compliments of the 'coach'" and went away.

Her heart skipped a beat. She knew! She looked again to where he had been dining in the corner. The table was empty. She looked around. He was gone.

Outside a horse neighed. Then she heard hoof beats.

She felt a warm hand on her own hand. Her husband was back. Seeing the flushed look on her face, he asked whether she was feeling well.

Absentmindedly, she said: "Yes."

He ordered another bottle of Pinot and led her to the dance floor. As they danced close, her head on his shoulder, she stared at the glass of shikhanji at their table....

The End.

Jaipur to Pilani by Rajasthan Roadways

January '85

Ajmeri reaches the Jaipur Bus Stand at 9.00 pm, dropped off by his uncle. He says bye to him and waits for him to go so that he can have a smoke. He carries his Aristocrat suitcase to the ticket counter, carefully trying to avoid stepping on people sleeping on the ground. He buys his ticket and walks up to the bus. He gets a coolie to climb on to the roof of the bus with his suitcase and secure it to the railing with his handkerchief. Another smoke, and he walks up to his seat. The seat number is painted in Hindi. He gets a window seat.

The driver jumps in through his door and starts the bus. The conductor shouts: Sikar, Jhunjhunu, Chirawa, Pilani. He is trying to get more passengers.

The bus starts moving, the conductor keeps shouting, banging the side of the bus. A bigger than normal bang signals to the driver to stop, as there is a potential new passenger. However, the passenger's destination is not on their route. So, with a few choice abusive words (Bawli g***, etc) the normal banging resumes. The banging continues until they are out of the bus stand.

The conductor begins his round checking tickets, manoeuvring between passengers and luggage in the aisles. A few arguments ensue about the age of some kids whose parents have bought 'half' tickets. Normalcy returns as the conductor makes his way to the driver's cabin. The lights are put off and the conductor lights up two beedis (leaf rolled smokes); one for himself, one for the driver. The driver puts on the 'tape recorder' playing Hindi movie songs.

First stop is Chomu. Ajmeri gets down for a quick smoke, also to check no one has 'downloaded' his suitcase. He does this at every stop!

The grimy bus window makes a constant rattling sound next to him, and as it rattles, it keeps sliding open letting in icy cold air. Every few minutes, he has to slide it back. The guy next to him starts snoring and his head starts falling on Ajmeri's shoulders. Ajmeri is an old hand at this. He no longer wakes him up to ask him to sit straight; all that does is that the fellow-passenger falls asleep right away and resumes his head lolling. Instead, Ajmeri elbows him really hard. When he looks up, Ajmeri pretends to be asleep. That ensures he avoids lolling on Ajmeri for another hour at least and blesses the person on the other side with his intimacy.

They arrive at Sikar. Ajmeri needs to pee. He gets down from the bus and walks off into the darkness. His fingers are frozen, and he finds it really hard to open the zip. He gulps down a glass of hot chai and gets back into the bus. It is near midnight now and freezing cold. The guy next to him has a blanket on his lap. Ajmeri would pay a fortune to share it, smelly as it is.

On the other side of the guy next to Ajmeri, is his wife with a baby in the lap. The baby has been good so far, but the music or the smell of the beedis, or his dad lolling on its mum's shoulders has annoyed it. It starts wailing. The mother tries to rock it to sleep. The guy across the aisle rattles his keys at the baby. The father ignores it all and sleeps away. Then there is a shout from some guy at the back of the bus: "boba dey." (give it a breast). The mother ignores him; the guy repeats: "boba dey." The father then gets upsets and says: Kaun bol raha hai? (Who's speaking?). Some other guy taking advantage of the darkness pipes in: "Doosra isko dey." (give him the other breast). The whole bus starts laughing. The embarrassed mother gives the baby what it wants and peace returns.

At Mukundgarh, the driver gets down and has a meal. Ajmeri can see him downing a quarter bottle of liquor in one shot. Ajmeri buys a 'donna' (bowl made of leaves) of daal (lentil) pakoras; so do a few others in the bus. A couple of hours later the atmosphere in the bus smells of the aftereffects of the pakoras going through the digestive cycles. Ajmeri longs for the smell of beedi smoke to override it.

After that, the bus passes through Nawalgarh, Jhunjhunu, and Chirawa...and it is the last stretch to Pilani. Ajmeri is just dreaming of his bed in his room and the thick rajai (quilt) and the room heater.

He arrives at Nutan bus stand, gets his suitcase down, haggles with a rickshaw wallah, and rides into the campus. As soon as the rickshaw crosses the campus gate, the air is suddenly warmer. He goes to his room, puts on the room heater, changes quickly and jumps into bed.

He has arrived home; his home for the next 4 months.

(by 1986, Rajasthan Roadways had 'deluxe' buses... A much more pleasant experience...maybe?).

2-in-one

August 1986.

Rajasthan Roadways Bus Stand

Sindhi Camp, Jaipur

9.30 pm

Two 83 batch BITSians boarding the night bus to Pilani.

SR: "Cigarette hai kya?" (do you have a cigarette?). "My dad has gone back home. I can smoke now."

Ajmeri: "I have only five. We'll need it for the trip. Let's share one."

After a while, Ajmeri: "Have you put your suitcase on top of the bus and tied it?"

SR: "Yes. I have put it on top. No need to tie it."

Ajmeri: "Ok then."

SR: "My dad bought me a new Phillips 2-in-1. 50 watts. I got some new taped cassettes too."

Ajmeri: "Wow!!! We can use it for our next booze party."

The bus slowly leaves the depot. The road is quite bumpy,

full of potholes. Suddenly someone asks the driver to stop. A rickshaw wallah is furiously chasing the bus, gesticulating with all his might. The bus stops. We hear that someone's suitcase has fallen off the roof of the bus. The rickshaw wallah had picked it up and given chase.

SR: "Bloody @&$&@!!! They just delay the bus!!!"

Conductor: "Yeh kiska suitcase hai?" (Whose suitcase is this?)

SR: "Hope the owner identifies it soon so that we can get moving."

Ajmeri: "Looks like your suitcase."

SR: Yes, it is @&$@&!!!

SR goes up the roof and ties up the suitcase this time.

Next morning, Pilani.

SRK opens his suitcase. The 2-in-1 is now a 20-in-1.

First day of the semester after the summer vacation

Take a rickshaw from Nutan bus stand into the campus. Collect your crate from the common room. Go on to discover your new room. Check your chair and the rest of the furniture. Open out your essential stuff like mattress, bed sheets, toiletries, poster of Madhubala. Check whether any of the glass windowpanes need 'brown papering/newspapering'. Find out whether any of your new wingees have arrived as yet, show off your new 2-in-1, take a long walk to the mess dreading a change back to mess food, greeting friends exaggeratedly loudly (machaan, BC,MC, etc.), chance to give the lungs full exercise after two and half months of civilised behaviour. Leaving mess food half-finished and going to the nearest rehri for a samosa, gajar halwa, followed by a shikhanji, have a smoke without fear of parents/ siblings/ neighbours/ relatives watching. Walk over to Nutan, relax in the moodas, with a tea and a few smokes, watching Haryana Roadways, DTC and Rajasthan Roadways coming in with their load of BITSians. Checking out the eye-catching freshers. Rickshaw wallahs doing roaring business, especially with the first timers. Call it a night and walk back to the bhawan, lying on the wooden bed and thinking of the comfy bed at home, thinking of the next holidays…drifting off to sleep…back to the grind the next day…

Cricket

He heard some 'noise' coming from his Bhawan. He walked up to see what was happening. There was a cricket match on in the quadrangle.

It was quite a scene. He had read about cricket being played in the English countryside with its class and tradition. This was better.

Thak-Thak, the all-rounder was batting. Cool, composed, he watched as the opposing captain set the field. He twirled his bat, whilst his cheer squad in silk dhotis shouted encouragement.

At the non-striker's end was the batting genius from BARC, Mumbai, affectionately called 'Tendlya'.

Tendlya leaned on his favourite bat, twirling his pride…his moustache. He had already worked out the climate conditions, the bowling assets of the opposing team and his mind was calculating the run rate after every ball. His sidee Guppy was the next batsman in. Tendlya and Guppy had played for many years for their school; so, knew each other's game well.

Perched on the balcony on the floor above, Neel kept an eye on the game making sure no side deals were being done. Shams from the 85 batch was getting ready to bowl, vigorously 'shining' the tennis ball on his pyjamas, leaving a green sheen on them.

Short Dada was umpiring. He was seated on the small chair at the non-striker's end nursing a Hayward's 5000 and a bada (big) Gold Flake, looking very lethargic. However, the moment there was a run, he jumped up and scooted from the chair as the throw came in.

There was a group of Hyderabadis waiting to use the court/ quadrangle. They were practicing with mock run ups, mock diving catches, mock square cuts…and loud mock appeals!

At the boundary, KV guy was 'fielding'. He had been roped in last minute with a promise of a 'shake' in C'Not as the fielding team was short of numbers. He stood there under his mop of freshly Clinic Plus shampooed hair. He stood there irrespective of who was at the crease, over after over.

Occasionally the captain shouted: "KV guy, ready?" KV guy whispered to himself in reply: "WTF..."

II.

Watching these two stalwarts bat was attracting a crowd of cricket connoisseurs.

Jay and Nod were on their way to play golf in their make-do golf cart (a rickshaw). Dressed in tweed caps and checked slacks, holding onto their gold bags, they bade their buggy driver to "tarry a bit".

Pras was doing a lap of the bhawan for his Sunday afternoon constitutional. He was reading his latest acquisition from the fiction section of the library. He put a wet finger at the page he was reading and leaned against a neem tree to watch.

Four MBites on their way back from the Swimming Pool, riding doubles on their bikes, stopped as well, hair dripping wet; Crowning Glory and chlorine scents wafting from them. Jay bade his golf cart driver to move the buggy closer to these four, ostensibly for a better view to watch the match.

Kolls was walking his dogs and stopped by the neem tree where Pras was leaning. The dogs sniffed at the tree enquiringly.

The Tom Brady look-alike was returning after an intense solo training session. He stopped as well, a 'slightly' deflated ball in one hand, silver helmet in the other.

BioS walked by on his way back from the mess, peering at a seed of roasted saunf (fennel seed) through a monocle. He stopped and leaned against one of the wing pillars.

Gor, Chor and Rai paused their heated argument about 'Allahabadi grandeur' vs 'Lucknavi Tehzeeb'. They passed around the Paan Parag and turned to watch.

A couple of mess servants who had stepped out from the

backdoor of the mess for a quick smoke, stopped to observe as well. Service in the mess was affected.

A camel cart which had travelled all morning from the Jat's village, stopped to watch. The camel appreciated the break.

Tall Dada walked out from the bogs in a short, skimpy, threadbare towel. He had to weave his way through the crowd to his room. Not wearing his glasses didn't help. He saw Short Dada and asked his Assamese buddy: "Time Kimaan?"

Short Dada looked at his Rolex and replied: 2.30 'BC'!

Opening Batsman

Tendlya rushed to Skylab from the workshop. The workshop had been hot, the 3 pm sun outside was hotter.

He ducked into M block, past ARC, past the library, Audi, S block...into Sky...as fast as his short legs could carry him.

Someone had told him that Lambi usually came alone to Sky at this time to 'study'.

Lambi was tall. Tendlya was not tall. However, he had noticed her occasionally stopping her bike and watching him practising his cricket strokes in the nets by the gym. He was smitten!

Meanwhile at Sky, he met his teammate Thak-Thak and they ordered a shikhanji each. Soft spoken and mild mannered Thak-Thak suggested they take a seat. Tendlya appeared distracted. He kept looking towards S block for her to arrive.

The shikhanji was down to the ice shards and lime seeds; when Pappu (who seemed to know about affairs, failed affairs, imaginary affairs and crushes) signalled with a wink to Tendlya; she was coming.

She had her chunni shielding her head from the hot sun. As she lithely walked up, Tendlya whipped out a small comb from his hip pocket and hurriedly combed his USP: his moustache!

After the rain

She stood under the neem tree on the pavement outside the Ashok Bhawan new wing.

It was a humid evening. After a few long hot weeks, there had been a downpour late that afternoon. The dried ground had hungrily absorbed the water.

Except for a few puddles on the tarred road, it was as if the rain hadn't happened. The dust had settled though, leaving the air clear. Invisible steam still arose from the now cooled pavement stones as they changed colour from a wet soggy grey to the clear sunny white lime paint.

It was humid, but the humidity was disappearing fast. It was as if nature had delivered an unplanned downpour and was rapidly trying to cover all evidence it had happened.

While she waited, she looked into her Jaipuri bag/ jhola. The sun reflected off the tiny mirror pieces sewn into the bag; the light from the sun filtering through the neem leaves. It also reflected off the puddles.

She was waiting for him to emerge out of his room on the ground floor. Some of her wingees cycled past on the way to the swimming pool.

She waved.

Some rickshaw wallahs passed by, looking at her meaningfully, subtly trying to get her attention by ringing their cycle bells.

She waited.

She looked at her toes. The nail polish was wearing off. Her payals (anklets) gleamed in the late evening sunlight. One of her sandals had a slight speck of dried mud just behind the heel. She rubbed it off against the neem tree.

She wished she could walk up to his room door and knock. Maybe he would be out quicker.

Nagarji passed by pushing his rattling, overladen cart along with his chottu. He parked it opposite the gym for the evening. She must stop by later for a samosa.

Nagarji nodded at her. Chottu turned back and smiled at her. She smiled back.

A sudden gentle breeze came through. It ruffled her curls and her clothes. She felt a sweet shiver, as if she had been tickled.

She reached into her jhola, took out Barbara Cartland novel, leaned against the tree and read.

She felt good.

II.

He came out finally. His green eyes smiled. Oiled curly hair, strong smell of Old Spice after-shave.

She liked the fragrance of the Old Spice. He had hardly any facial hair. She wondered why he used after shave. It didn't bother her too much.

They set off to C'Not on the back road. Staff quarters lined one side of the street, the gym grounds on the other.

He set off at a fast pace. The flat of his chappals slapping the underside of his heels, set up a steady beat.

The evening sun was suddenly warm. She covered her head with her chunni. She spoke a lot. He didn't talk much; just occasionally making eye contact. His smiling eyes and dimpled cheeks reassured her. He was listening.

Passing one of the staff quarters, he stopped. A new raised veggie bed had been recently planted. They could still smell the fresh manure rich soil.

In the midst of the bed sat a golden retriever all muddied up, comfortably ensconced in the dip he had dug. A few saplings lay around. The retriever looked at them with large naughty eyes. His tongue hung out panting.

The couple exchanged smiles and walked on.

The dog turned around to a more comfortable position, scratched behind his ear, put his head on his front paws and dozed off.

Daffodils

He sat on the bench in Skylab and took in the crisp early spring air. The daffodils around him were blooming. Yellow was her favourite colour. Maybe, when he saw her walking into Sky, he would pluck a few and give her a posy.

He adjusted his Ray-ban Aviators on his chiselled nose and rubbed his strong jaw. He waited. A few couples and some groups passed by. They were all juniors.

He waited.

A few sparrows chased each other from tree to tree, flying low; one of them nearly clipped his neatly groomed hair. He ducked.

He waited.

A squirrel paused by a tree. Keeping a wary eye on him, it nibbled on a nimboli. (fruit of a neem tree).

He waited.

He saw her parking her bicycle. She was wearing a yellow top and skinny tights.

He hurriedly collected a few long-stemmed daffodils and waited.

She was lost from sight for a couple of minutes. Maybe she was looking for him.

He stood up. He saw her. He waved.

She didn't see him. She wasn't looking for him.

She was walking towards AB. AB stood there dressed in his gold kurta, holding a bunch of yellow roses. She walked up to him, graciously accepted the roses. She rose on the tips of her toes, and brushed cheeks with him.

Meanwhile, on the bench, he sat back, tossed the daffodils on the ground and wondered...

Love on a cassette

This happened in his third year. Gol Guppa had an interesting situation. Well, Gol Guppa was a late riser, and missed breakfast most days. On the other hand, Ajmeri, his wingee was in the gym at 5:00 am each day, 6 days a week. Sundays, he would sleep in, but would make it to the mess before 9:00 am for his French toast.

Gol Guppa had a girlfriend in his hometown, a Year 10 student. He had struck up a conversation at a bus stop whilst the damsel waited for her school bus, and from then on she was madly in love. Let's call her Pani Puri.

Pani Puri was lazy, and instead of writing letters, she would record cassettes with her love messages and mail it to Gol Guppa. Gol Guppa would listen to her cassettes just before going to bed on his 40 Watt 2-in-1 PMPO.

All was well.

It so happened that Gol Guppa developed a platonic friendship with an '84 MBite. Let's call her Samosa.

Samosa had this habit of coming to Gol Guppa's bhawan every Sunday at 10:00 am, standing on the road and calling for Gol Guppa. Gol Guppa was lost in sleep, and after a few attempts she would call Ajmeri, knowing they were friends and he was awake. Ajmeri would then walk over to Gol Guppa's room and try and wake him up. Gol Guppa would ignore him for a long time. Ajmeri's efforts were hampered because he couldn't use normal 'effective' wake-up language, because Samosa was within earshot.

This was seriously impacting Ajmeri's Sundays. Besides wasting his time, he had to shed the wrapped towel around his waist (his usual Sunday room wear) for decent attire, so as not to offend Samosa. He tried telling Gol Guppa (in effective language) and Samosa (in decent language) to come to some sort of arrangement which would mutually work for them, to no avail…

…until one Sunday, when circumstances and naughtiness combined.

This Sunday, as usual Samosa arrived. The previous night there has been a romantic flick in the Audi, and Ajmeri was still dreaming of Juhi C.

He heard Samosa call Gol Guppa a few times, and then inevitably call him. Ajmeri pulled on his pants and T shirt. Samosa was wearing a white salwar kurta. Her hair was wet (must have just had a shower); the enticing vapours of Crowning Glory wafted over. Her cheeks were Punjabi pink and ruddy. It was drizzling and the drops got caught up in her hair and kurta. Sigh!

Ajmeri walked up to Gol Guppa's room. Gol Guppa had left the door unlatched. Ajmeri looked at the slob lying on the bed. He looked at Juhi....oops, Samosa. He looked at the 2-in-1....and had a brain fade/snap.

He hit play, turned the volume up to the full 40-Watt capacity, and walked back to his room.

The wing and Samosa heard Pani Puri's endearing voice and loving speech. Gol Guppa soon woke up, swore, cursed, saw Samosa, apologized, etc. etc....

The Sunday morning episodes ceased. Gol Guppa didn't speak to Ajmeri for three days.

They shared a ciggy on the fourth day and made up. Samosa found a new friend.

All was well again.

Holi

212 Gandhi.

He woke up in the middle of the night with a strange feeling of wetness.

At first, he thought it was the bhang.

The wetness became uncomfortable and he woke up throwing off the sheets and put on the ceiling light.

What he saw, sent his pulse racing, his heart pounding. He had not only wet himself; the liquid was red!

Then he saw something sticking out of his pyjama pocket. He had slept with his 'loaded' pitchkari (water gun).

Relieved, he chided himself...kya rey Mangey!

A Summer's day

August 1986.

It had been a hot day. The tar on the roads had semi-melted.

The dedicated ones had gone to the Institute walking on the pavements, avoiding the tarred roads, covering their heads from the hot sun with their notebooks. Even the trip at lunch to the mess, and back, was like stepping into an oven.

A few sat under the neem tree opposite the gym through the day, sampling copious amounts of shikhanjis. The shady areas in Sky had people lazily lounging.

By evening the sun had set, but the breeze that rustled through the branches, and the bhawan wings, that swirled dust clouds on the gym grounds and behind the messes, was still hot.

In the p wing upstairs in Bhagirath, Maltese had decided to stay in his room all day; he had taken the longer route to the mess for lunch, avoiding the sun. Maltese looked after his complexion. The fan had roared in his room all day.

After an early dinner, he had a shower, collected an old, much viewed mag from his sidee and settled down in his room to lie down. The smell of room cooked Maggi wafted in his nostrils and he was tempted to take his spoon and walk to the source of the smell. He didn't; it was too hot.

The shower, the soft pyjamas, the Thursday grub of cutlets and bread and tomato ketchup, the dreamy pictures in the mag, the breeze from the fan... they all conspired to put him to an early sleep.

It was one of those days when the hot sun had sapped even the most extreme extroverts of their energy. It was a quiet evening in Bhagirath. People walked around topless in shorts, lungis and pyjamas. The lungis were wrapped and unwrapped frequently; it supposedly cooled the lower body.

Maltese woke up in a sweat in the middle of the night. His fan had stopped. He opened his window, but that didn't help.

After a while, he dragged his bed out to the balcony. He positioned the top of his bed over the balcony wall and rested the other end on his small chair. He put on his mattress and bed cover, pillow and a sheet to cover him.

As he lay, a gentle cooler breeze had started and ruffled through his curls. The sky was full of stars, blurred to him as he had left his glasses in his room. The gusts gently lifted the edges of his bed sheet occasionally and lapped his ankles.

He slept. The moon peaked at him through the neem branches, casting slow moving shadows on his fair complexion.

He didn't notice.

He slept.

Intolerance

A quartet of Illad freshers from Shankar went to the Chief Warden to complain. They had been referring to the steel/aluminium glasses in the mess 'tumblers' and the Himachali mess servants had looked at them with derision. They felt there was intolerance in the Shankar Vyas mess. The mess secretary had suggested they go back to Tamil Nadu.

The next lot of the Chief Warden's visitors were some militant MBites. They felt that the 11 pm curfew was intolerant to their gender. The MB warden had offered to send them to Balika Vidyapeeth where there was a 7 pm curfew.

Khandu went alone to the Chief Warden. Every time he sang at the music nights; people banged chairs. The organisers had asked him to busk at Nutan instead. Intolerant audience!

The Telegus were upset that the MBites had chosen a non-Telegu for a mess secretary, unlike all the other boys' hostels. The non-Telegu MBites had asked them to go to RTC X Roads! They felt that the MBites were intolerant!

The Choms were a minority in their own state. They were clubbed with the locals. The others were intolerant and asked them to go back to....

...to....

...Rajasthan!

They thought they were already there!

Medical check-up at Induction

January, 1984.

They were sent for medicals to Birla Sarvajanik Hospital, as part of the induction for new students.

Ajmeri goes with his wingees from a 'particular' state in North India. He stands in a queue behind two brothers.

One is done, the other one approaches the doctor.

Doctor asks him: Are you brothers?

They both say: Yes.

Doctor asks: Are you sure?

They say: Yes.

Doctor asks: Same father and same mother?

Both are offended.

One of them: Kya Matlab? (What do you mean?).

The other wingees from the same state sense something is wrong, so they gather around the doctor, clutching at their gamchas (cloth scarves that doubles as towels).

The doctor senses danger.

In a meek voice he says: There is a three-month difference between your dates of birth.

Some silence...

Then the brothers say: So?

The doctor says: nothing, sab theek hai (all good); and signs off the documents.

Ajmeri is next. The doctor looks at him.

Ajmeri says he's not related, not even from the same state.

The doctor signs off without examining his documents anyway.

A short football career

Around February of 1984, after the ragging had died down, the second semmer from Shankar (Ajmeri) decided to wander over to the sports ground to seek adventure. His Bihari wingees were involved in high level politics and sports was the last thing on their agenda.

He put on his school PT white shorts and school PT white keds and ventured over to the field. Wasn't a long walk from the Shankar back wing. There he found Kums, a first semmer, practising his goal keeping with a mess servant kicking the ball to him.

As the second semmer walked the boundary line, the ball drifted towards him, and he kicked it back to Kums. By some strange mix of aerodynamics, Bernoulli's principle and chance, the ball took a 'Beckhamisque' trajectory and floated over the head of Kums into the goal!

Kums was impressed. In those days of 5-3-2-1 combinations, apparently the BITS first year team was looking for a 'left-out'. Since the second semmer had kicked with his left foot, he was instantly drafted in.

It turned out that it was the last goal he scored in BITS football.

Soon there was the BITS inter-year football tournament, and someone introduced another second semmer to the group. This one had come to BITS as a state sprint champion and had the intimidating presence of a Ronaldo. Well in the first game, Ajmeri got substituted at half-time by the sprinter. Everyone watched in awe as the sprinter bulldozed through the opposition defences and left it in tatters. The 83 batch won the inter-year that year largely due to the sprinter.

That was the end of Ajmeri's brief football career. He found his way to the gym and spent half of his waking hours there for the next 3 years.

Weightlifting Captain

Ajmeri would like to put on record his thanks to two 'seniors' JS and NG who, without knowing it, had a huge impact on his life.

Ajmeri joined Pilani as a second semmer, the sole person in his batch doing Museum Studies.

When he first went to the gym, there was JS, a huge guy (he was the Volleyball Captain) doing 30 kg bench presses. Being Ajmeri's first time, he tried to change the bar to 5 kg, JS didn't let him until he had finished his routine. He then made a snide comment to another guy: "Aaj kal school ke bacchon ko admit kar rahe hain." (they are admitting school kids to BITS these days). Can't blame him, Ajmeri was a puny 40 kgs and 5'5".

However, over the course of two years with 6 hours in the gym 6 days a week, 4-6 raw eggs in the mess every morning, Ajmeri had developed into a competitive bantam weight. He represented Jhunjhunu district at the Rajasthan Powerlifting opens in 1986. He was BITS weightlifting captain and was bench pressing up to 90 kgs. He had an active BITS bodybuilding team in training as well.

Sometime in 1986, JS came in one day to the gym in the middle of Ajmeri's routine, saw the weights loaded up on the bench press and looked at Ajmeri. Ajmeri asked him to wait. JS quietly left. Ajmeri wondered if he recognised the puny kid about whom he had made that snide comment.

NG was the Weightlifting captain the year Ajmeri joined, and he had managed to obtain funds to install new equipment in the gym, besides putting up posters from Arnie Schwarzenegger's routines.

These posters were Ajmeri's only 'coach'. Far removed from gyms these days, with coaches, supplements, etc.

Tarzan in the gym

Ajmeri had a chela (disciple) in the gym; an 85-batcher called Lambu.

There was an 82 batcher (let's call him Tarzan, you'll know why shortly), who used to visit the gym for brief but memorably annoying visits. Those who knew the old gym will recollect that towards the right side there were roman rings and a rope suspended from the ceiling. The rope was meant for climbing. However, Tarzan loved to swing on the rope as a giant pendulum with a radius of 20 feet. He would swing into the right wall, bounce off, gain momentum and swing right back. The length of his arc was 40 feet in a gym of 100 feet length. It was very disconcerting when one was doing heavy weights, to see someone swinging in your peripheral vision.

Ajmeri warned Tarzan a couple of times but being a 'senior'

he ignored it. One fine day, when he swung too close for comfort, Ajmeri asked his chela Lambu to whack Tarzan on the backside (it sounds more 'pleasant' in Hindi of course, 'GPL').

To his surprise Lambu, did it.

That fixed the issue.

Valentine's Day

February 14ᵗʰ, 1985.

According to unconfirmed Twitter feeds and other Social Media updates, there had been reports of concerning incidents involving the delivery of mail to Meera Bhawan.

Traditionally, around this time (approaching Valentine's Day); there was an increase of mail, especially greeting cards, to MB.

Since Feb 11th, a group of 'J' supporters, had been stopping the postman at the bend of the road approaching MB near the temple. They had been stamping all the cards with, 'With Love from J'.

J was interviewed late night by campus sleuths and the Chief Warden, but he denied any knowledge of the incident and condemned it, unequivocally.

He said this was a conspiracy from the K gang to defame him.

In a related incident, B reported to his close wingees, that he was accosted as he made his way to MB with a yellow rose for C at 6.30 am.

(He wanted to get in early to avoid unnecessary attention, and C was usually in her best mood in the morning, just after her walk in the garden.)

B said that he was stopped by an unidentified J supporter who stamped the note on which B had lovingly scribbled the poem 'Roses are red, violets are blue…. etc,'; with a 'With Love from J'!

C wasn't happy!

II.

Feb 15th, 1985

P had had to wait an entire day because of the new rules for visitors to MB.

He felt he was disadvantaged, as he had an ID ending in an odd number. Visitors to MB were being carefully monitored. People with IDs ending in odd numbers could only visit on odd numbered calendar dates and vice versa.

The rule was ostensibly to reduce emotional and hormonal pollution in the general area.

P, a Hyderabadi, wore his new Chermas jeans with the 'zari' embroidery around the back pockets, his 'Chiranjeevi' flashing LED lights belt, a yellow shirt and trudged to MB.

In his hand, he carried a daisy with odd numbered petals.

III.

Feb 9th, 1985

BioS had bought his pink lacy Valentine's Day card.

He had written a note; not too senti, not too impersonal either.

Now, the hard part would start. Visits to the library, Sky, C'Not, temple, workshop. It was agonising: "Why is courting so hard?!" he thought to himself.

Usually it came to him the morning of the 14th after a restless night's sleep. That's when he decided whom to send the card to.

This year it was for Sunny.

It just felt right!

IV.

Feb 14th, 1986
5:30 pm

AB, RG, AM and SG sat at Blue Moon in C'Not. It was AM's treat.

They ordered samosas.

Whilst they waited, they talked boisterously, eyes darting at the MB bicycles that swooped in and out of C'Not.

Sanjay and Sanjay and Sanjay and Sanjay had walked in together each holding a long-stemmed yellow rose. Unknown to the other Sanjays, Sanjay had a bar of Cadbury's chocolates as well.

Meanwhile, four pairs of steaming hot samosas in white saucers with steel spoons arrived. The smell of the samosas filled the chilly February evening air.

AM's tummy made a strange welcoming gurgling sound.

They liberally poured the sauce and green chutney and proceeded to eat.

No one spoke as the samosas were crushed, broken into, the crusty bits rendered soft in the mix of sauce and green chutney. An occasional pea would try to break away but was quickly captured by the steel spoon and consumed.

In a little over five minutes, the deed was done. The white saucers were left with the tell-tale evidence of a gastronomic massacre in the form of streaks of red and green. The samosas had disappeared as if they had never existed.

A few crumbs remained on AB's moustache and a spot of red sauce on AM's white kurta.

As they drank water from the plastic jugs, they noticed that the Sanjays and their roses were no longer there.

V.

February 14th, 1987

It was the season of romance in the campus.

Brooke Shields had captured imaginations in the last Saturday Audi flick 'Blue Lagoon'. 'Going Steady' was playing in Blue Moon. Dabba had 'QSQT' drawing large crowds, while Nihali Chowk was having reruns of …'a special movie'.

Messages had cropped across the campus, saying 'I Love S'!

Some tree trunks in Skylab had the message engraved. Some desks in the library and M42 and S12 and C37 had the message carved onto them.

It got bolder by the day. As Diro arrived to work one morning, he found a post-it note with the message on his inbox. He dismissed it by saying he already knew that. His wife's name commenced with an S.

An A4 sheet with the message was slipped under a EEE Prof''s door. He thought it was from his wife and beamed extra bright all day.

It was written in chalk on the steps leading to the swimming pool. The girls studiously avoiding stepping on the 'S', as it could be a friend.

One of the rickshaw wallahs woke up from his afternoon snooze, parked outside the campus gates to find the message sprayed on the rear of his rickshaw between OK and TATA.

It got serious when the Chief Warden's name plate outside his chamber was turned around and the message was found on it. Campus sleuths were pressed into operation to find out who the lovesick perpetrator was.

Across the campus, it became the hot topic of discussion as people tried to guess who the 'I' and 'S' were.

Many theories were floating around. All the girls with 'S' as a first name or as a last name were monitored closely; including who called on them at MB, who sat beside them in class, any stalkers, etc.

It went on for a couple of weeks; the messages kept appearing in new places. The person writing them continued to remain a mystery.

MB woke up one morning to a surprise.

Punch cards had been slipped under each door during the night, with 'I love S'...

The mystery has never been solved.

VI.

Feb 14th, 2018

They sat in the darkened restaurant by the window. The sole candle on the table cast a glow on her rosy cheeks. He was thinking this was the night.

They looked into each other's eyes as they waited for their food to be served. The candlelight flickered in their eyes, driving flames of youthful passion.

Suddenly she tensed up as she saw a couple entering the restaurant.

He asked her what was wrong.

She replied: "My mum's here 83A3PS1xx." I wonder who that man is with her.

He turned to look and froze: "It's my dad 83B3A4xx!"

What kind of wife will I have?

A conversation happened in Bhagirath new wing upstairs during the second semester 1986. It was about what kind of wife one would want to have.

The discussion was held after Sunday lunch, including cassata ice-cream followed by saunf and the mandatory 'chotta' Gold Flake.

The participants ranged from some who had had multiple girlfriends, guys who had friends behind the wall (Meera Bhawan) and then guys who had never had a girl 'friend'.

The conversation was more graphic and more to do with the physical side of things. The philosophers and theorists got drowned out by the 'experienced' ones.

It was a big unknown, with comments like: "My wife is out there somewhere at this very moment;" "l would like an open relationship with my wife"; "I'd never marry a BITSian" (apologies MB'ites); "I'd like to have a relationship, before I get married"; "Will I lose my freedom if I get married" thrown in…

What did come out was the excitement and the fear of being married one day.

As the discussion was taken over by the louder ones; the group slowly disintegrated with some going for an afternoon nap (hopefully dreaming of wedded bliss), and others relocating to BC (the canteen behind the bank).

Year of the Monkey

Ashu, Joy and Bals got up early that morning.

They polished their cameras, checked the batteries, mounted their cycles and rode up to their meeting point near the dairy farm (near the Gliding Club).

They met at 8.08 am and bowed and nodded to each other. They each wore Chinese silk tops. The tops were all red, however the flower and dragon motifs were a different.

Joy produced a 'lion' mask he had picked up from the Ana Sagar fair. Ashu had a curved, flexible neem twig attached behind him to his belt.

They lined up crouching: Joy leading with his mask; Bals next with his arms on Joy's shoulders, followed by Ashu with his arms on Bals' shoulders.

They gracefully leaped around the dairy farm fences, undulating in their leaps as they went.

The cows stopped feeding and watched in awe and fear. Later that evening, the cowherds were amazed that their teats were taut and unresponsive; milk production was minimal, they didn't know why.

At 8.38 am, the trio stopped their dance, bowed to each other again and cycled to the toy shop in Nutan.

They purchased stuffed monkeys.

Wrong call

Pony had spent all Saturday afternoon getting ready.

Salwar ironed, makeup done, hair neatly coiffured, perfume, lipstick in the bag, last touches of mascara.

The wingees knew something was up, they dared not ask what. They gathered in S's room and held a whispered conference trying to guess.

Then the call came; Nani's announcement: Sanjay for Pony!

The door slammed shut as Pony raced down the stairs and then composed herself walking ladylike to the Meera Bhawan gate.

S and the other wingees excitedly strained to catch a glimpse of Sanjay.

A minute later, they found Pony walking back to her room, looking a bit angry.

S arched her eyebrow enquiringly at her. Pony replied: Wrong Sanjay!

…Sometime later, in Ashok Bhawan.

There was a loud knocking on Louda's door. He opened the door to find an angry Sanjay.

Kya hua?

Saaley…humey kahaan bhej diya tumne?

MB bheja tha …kya hua… jaldi kyon aa gaya?

Jaldi? Hum apni white pant, peela T shirt pehenkar, jootey polish kar ke, kesh mein sarson ka tel daal ke, Old Spice ki poori seeshi laga ke, naya Rupa underwear pehen ke, snan kar ke, neem ke dantan se brush kar ke…tumhare keheney pe, MB gaya.

Phir kya Hua?

Kya hua? Woh aayee saj dhaj ke, lipstick, powder laga ke…humara dil speed pakad raha tha…phir woh angrezi mein boli…Wrong Sanjay…aur phir upar bhaag gayee…

Oh!

Vyas Meera Fête

Vyas and Meera Bhawan partnered on a fête every year. The 1986 fête was coming up.

Jay and S were putting up a tomato salad stall.

On the day before the fête, Jay hired a cycle and went to MB, picked S up, seated her on the carrier with two thelis (cloth bags) and rode up to Nutan.

S held Jay around the waist, quite genteelly.

They stopped at a cart selling tomatoes and parked the cycle.

S selected the tomatoes very carefully. Jay wanted to speed up the process, so he chose a couple of tomatoes and put them in the theli.

S inspected the tomatoes Jay and chosen. She wasn't happy with his selection and removed them.

Sometime later, impatient Jay selected a couple more.

S slapped him on the wrist.

II.

B and P walked up to the Vyas-Meera fête.

They had been planning this for over a month now. Neither of them lived in Vyas or Meera. In actual fact, they didn't care about the Vyas part of the equation anyway. The Vyasites main claim to fame was dwelling at the crossroads of the most intense evening traffic: Mandir, C'Not and Shiv Ganga lawns.

Anyway, short of budget, they had dinner in the mess, went to B's room, shared a quarter of Old Monk, pocketed another quarter for boosting courage later on, rehearsed their lines again and went off to the fete.

There was the regular atmosphere at the fête: music, food stalls, smokes; people wanting to be seen as 'cool'; the locals; the bhaiyyas and Biharis, and an occasional ghotu.

They looked around and found their target. A stall with 4 MBites, no Vyasites...and no customers.

They had a swig each off the Old Monk quarter, the courage rose exponentially; they walked up to the target stall and introduced themselves by the popular versions of their last names.

Next day, the chowki in Shankar caught up with the chowki in Vyas and mentioned how the chief warden had summoned two Saxenas to his office.

Fundraiser

It was that time of the year when S did a solo fund raiser for her alma mater.

The previous night a wicker basket had been delivered to the MB gate, and she sought the help of a couple of the wingees to carry it to her room. The wicker basket was quite full, neatly covered with a Rajasthani chunni.

She asked them to delicately place it in her room.

Early morning, she had a shower and washed off the mehndi. She then changed into a ghaghra choli with mirror work and accompanied by the two wingees walked up to the end of the road where the road curved towards the temple.

Here she removed the chunni off the wicker basket and spread it on the floor. The basket was full of local yellow-red tomatoes.

She then pulled her ghunghat low over her face and sat on her haunches and waited for customers. A local raddiwala donated a taraju (scales) for the cause with the half kilo and quarter kilo weights represented by suitable pebbles.

Another dropped off an earthen pot of drinking water.

Yet another placed a transistor next to her, playing Rajasthani folks songs including her favourite: pallo latke, gori ko pallo latke.

It was going to be a long day.

The sun rose and glittered off the mirrors in her choli, bedazzling passers-by.

A couple of rickshaw wallahs stopped by to sample her goods. They bought three tomatoes each. She expertly sliced them onto a newspaper sheet and liberally sprinkled salt and chilli powder. Soon business started picking up. People stopped, ate a couple of tomatoes, exchanged yarns with each other and then moved on. By mid-day, she was sold out.

She counted her takings for the day and safely stored it in the choli. She then stood up, put the chunni in the basket, placed the basket on her head and sashayed back to MB.

Encounter

August 4th, 1985

He heard sobbing from behind a neem tree in an isolated corner in Sky.

He had just sauntered around, collecting a shikhanji from Pappu, hoping to find anyone he knew to while away the two-hour break between classes.

The sobbing had drawn him towards the tree. He could see her sitting under the tree, her heads between her knees, a white chunni in her hands wiping away tears.

The sobbing was gentle. Next to her lay a couple of textbooks, a notebook, a pencil-case and her spectacles.

His first instinct was to walk away. He felt like an intruder.

He didn't know who she was, as her head was hidden between her knees. He tried to read the name on her notebook, but he was too far.

He looked around. There was no one in visual range. Maybe he should just let her have a cry.

He shuffled away, as quietly as he could. Just then, he heard a louder sob. He stopped and looked back at her.

She had lifted her head, but being behind her and the tree trunk, he still couldn't make out who she was. Her hair was a mess. She reached out for her glasses and the notebook.

She got out a pen and started writing in the notebook. She would have written a word or two, but then stopped. Another sob escaped. She put the pen down and wiped her smudged glasses with her chunni.

He watched mesmerised.

She stabbed the notebook with her pen; tore out the sheet and crunched it into a ball. She tossed it behind her. It landed next to his feet.

She became aware of him. Slowly she turned around. The sun glistened off her wet pink cheeks. A couple of neem leaves had lodged into her curls. The chunni was still around her neck, one end in her hands, wet.

He stood rooted to his spot, shikhanji in one hand, his own notebook in the other.

She stared at him. He tried to look into her eyes, the smudged glasses made it difficult.

A voice in his head said to walk away. She sobbed again and sunk her head in her knees. The sobs were stronger now.

He walked up to her and gently knelt beside her. Hesitatingly he touched her shoulders. She stiffened. She continued sobbing.

He wondered what to do next.

He saw a large shadow fall on them. He looked back; his arm came of her shoulder in a jiffy…

A couple of weeks later...

She sat on her bed dangling her legs playfully. The anklets clinked delicately against her soft ankles. The red nail polish glistened. She stared at the lines and serrations in her palms nestling in her lap and tried to find some meaning in them.

The Circuit Theory notebook lay besides her, her own notes now underlined in certain sections as she had done a coaching session with him in Sky.

In the gentle afternoon sun, she wondered if he had really been listening. He had missed the last few classes and asked her to help him catch-up. She had obliged.

After the two hours of intense coaching, he had offered to walk her back to MB. She had declined politely. She wanted to join her friends for dinner in the mess. She had cycled back, whilst he went back to Pappu to buy smokes.

Dinner had been the usual drab stuff; the conversation with her friends had been more animated. She got a few pointed, knowing looks from some bhawan mates. The two-hour session in Sky hadn't gone unnoticed. In this place, gossip was quick to take roots and blossom.

Most of her friends had a test the next day, so she was alone in her room.

She changed, put her stuff away, organised her books for next day, combed her hair, unknotting the fringes, cut off some split ends.

She looked at her notebook lying beside her again. She decided to call it a night.

As she folded the notebook shut, she noticed an unfamiliar shape drawn in the margin with an unfamiliar handwritten scribble below it.

The scribble read: Thanks

The shape was....

The next Saturday...

Kabali was screening in the Audi that night.

She had asked him to accompany her to the movie. She had

insisted, knowing that his shy studious self would be reluctant to go to a movie, let alone be accompanied by a girl. After Mod Phy class, she had begged, cajoled, pouted, nearly cried...the 'near crying' did it. Embarrassed at being seen with a crying girl in the busy M block corridors he has assented.

Since early that Saturday morning, his sidee 'Le Chat' had been most excited. She was from Chennai; Le Chat had drawn a life-size charcoal portrait of her on his wall. Some people felt that the portrait itself was a bit too voluptuous. Le Chat disagreed.

Le Chat was now transferring his advice to the 'invited one'. He first tried to get him to try his white bell bots; the 'invited one' was too tall. He then did a two-hour session teaching the 'invited one' to toss a cigarette in the air and catch it in his lips. After a 20 pack of Charms was wasted, Le Chat gave up.

Next, he tried to get the 'invited one' attired in a white silk dhoti. The 'invited one' had grown up in North Indian pyjamas and found the dhoti too airy and insecure.

Le Chat gave up.

She had asked the 'invited one' to meet up early. After a quick bread and stew dinner in the Shankar-Vyas mess, the 'invited one' attired in jeans, chappals and crumpled khadi kurta trudged to Meera Bhawan He collected his date and they began their leisurely stroll to the Audi. His mind was already on the Intro Phil test coming up.

She was excited!

They walked on the footpath. She tip toed on the edge of the footpath, prancing, singing Chinni Chinni Asha...

He had to keep pace with her, and occasionally support her when she nearly tripped off the footpath. Each time she held his arm to support herself from tripping, he felt a vague jolt in his heart.

His nonchalance was quickly giving way, he wasn't comfortable. As they neared Ram, she became conscious as well. She held on to his arm, he tried to gently break free.

Naughtily she put her hand in his kurta pocket. The weather had been humid all day, threatening to rain. Her closeness, the strong smell of the jasmine in her hair, the warmth of her forearms, the semi opaque chunni resting on her kurta added to the heat. He broke out into a sweat.

She looks up at him. She had nicknamed him 'BioS'. "BioS", she whispered. He looked straight ahead: "Yes."

She didn't say anything, just gently steered him to the now dark deserted Sky lawns…

Sunday afternoon.

208 Meera Bhawan

208 MB had a relaxing morning. She had skipped breakfast, instead she had nibbled on some protein bars. Early lunch had been delivered to her room by her favourite mess servant, Ramu. She had first eaten the cassata ice cream as it had already started to run on the steel plate, the three colours fusing together. Stupid Ramu had placed the ice-cream plate on top of the hot puris in the thaali. Whilst he had taken care to bring her the fully puffed puris, he had been a bit unsteady on his feet. The mutter-paneer had run into the puri compartment, making one of them soggy. Maybe the sight of 201 MB doing her Sunday yoga in the balcony had been what distracted him. 201 MB was a show-off!

Sigh!

After lunch, she had a quick nap, and then pulled out a chair into the corridor. She sat there and clipped and painted her nails. Because of the heavy lunch, she found it hard to bend and reach her toes. The thin silver anklets gleamed in the sunlight.

The smell of nail polish remover brought out her sidee. The sidee had a couple of long, deep sniffs from the nail polish remover bottle and went back to snooze.

After painting her nails, 208 MB collected the plastic water buckets (she always used two) which had now heated up to a generous temperature and marched to the bogs, towel on her shoulders.

She went back to collect her soap and shampoo and a change of clothes, entered the showers and latched the door behind her.

Three hours later, as she sat reading Linda Goodman in the corridor, a familiar buzz sounded.

The Blue Moon drone was hovering above, lowering a hot sealed pack.

She reached out and collected the pack and signed the receipt. The drone took off and flew back over the temple to land behind Blue Moon.

She unpacked the pack and ate her steaming hot Maggi noodles.

218 Malviya Bhawan

Kanhaiya woke up late that Sunday morning. He had missed breakfast.

Tightening his pyjama string, he got up from his bed and picked up the Indian Express which had been slid under his door earlier.

Through sleepy eyes, he looked at the headlines. He hadn't made the news.

His throat felt a bit hoarse after his impromptu speech the previous night in the RBM mess on the quality of chapattis. The chapattis were coarse and brittle.

Last night's chapattis had processed in his system overnight and now desired to exit.

Picking up the sports section of the Express, he pulled the religious string that he wore across his neck, positioned it over his right ear, bit off a piece of khaini, positioning it under his tongue, wrapped his gamcha around his neck, picked up a soap box and sauntered over to the bogs.

Jaipur to Pilani to MB to Shankar

It was the beginning of the semester. They had both arrived on the RSRTC evening bus at Jaipur bus stand. Although the bus was labelled on the sides as 'Semi Luxury, Non-Stop, Air Conditioned, Pilot: Ratan Lal ji, Chirawa waale'; it had stopped frequently and seemingly for every man, woman, kid and their belongings on the way. The bus had reached Nutan past midnight, and everyone, except one rickshaw guy, had gone home.

They were forced to share the rickshaw. Yuppie heard Imli arguing and bargaining with the beedi smoking rickshaw wallah in the harsh light of the Nutan Bus stand, among the water puddles. He was impressed and felt something akin to love at first sight. She bargained for both to be dropped; she first at Meera, him on the way back, at Shankar. They loaded their suitcases on the footrest. Imli with the agility of a langur, climbed up the seat. The conscientious rickshaw wallah respecting the fairer sex, seated Yuppie on the folded hood of the rickshaw behind Imli. That had been the defining moment in their relationship and had set the parameters for subsequent encounters.

As they entered the campus, Yuppie felt it was a homecoming, even though he was entering the campus backwards. As they turned the corner around Shankar, he looked furtively at his room, his warm bed and rajai, the Kylie Minogue poster on his wall and the collection of Wall Street Journals at his bedside.

The rickshaw drifted on. Imli had a conversation going with the rickshaw wallah about the dry season, the price of wheat and tomatoes, the prospects of the local Janata Party member in the next municipal election.

Occasionally, Yuppie thought about joining the conversation, but so enamoured was he of this 'lady' and her wealth of knowledge, he kept quiet.

They reached MB. Yuppie helped her to the gate with her suitcase. Imli looked him in the eye and shook hands with him (a firm military grip) and walked away.

Yuppie reverently occupied the seat Imli had vacated on the rickshaw. As they made their way towards Shankar, he gazed at the bright stars through the gaps in the canopy of the neem trees.

He felt something soft and fragrant on the seat beside him. There was a small handkerchief, quaintly embroidered with an 'I'.

He then realised; he didn't know her name…

Autograph signing day at Meera Bhawan

A table had been moved from the mess to under a tree just inside the MB gate.

There was a meandering queue of freshers, some of them who had woken up at 4 am, showered, shampooed, hair straightened, faces…done, etc.

The previous day there had been trips to the stationary shops in C'Not and Nutan to buy autograph books. They queued up now, holding their books and colourful pens, close to their chests.

P had been allowed access inside MB. He set up his camera, to get pictures of the autograph seekers with the autographers. P was a paragon of efficiency and had arrived dutifully at 7.45 am; 15 minutes before the signing was to start.

The signing table had been scrubbed clean by the mess crew, and all remnants of sambhar, rice, cassata, black daal, milk, coffee and tea had been erased to the best ability of the wash cloths and the arms and reach of those involved in the cleaning.

P dug into his bag of props and placed a few plastic flowers on the table.

There had been a debate by the organisers about whether the autographers should be seated on a mess bench; but the best cleaning efforts did not bring the benches up to any standard of required glamour the occasion demanded. There was also the health and safety risk, that some of the well-worn benches had occasionally extended a sliver, which caused wardrobe malfunctions and/or occasionally pinched sensitive areas. So, three chairs had been commandeered from fresher's rooms from the first floor. There were two short chairs (armchairs) whilst the third one was the normal, higher, desk chair as one of the autographers wasn't tall enough.

The three strolled in at 8.45 am. Nobody really expected them to be there at 8.00 am, however the wait had built up excitement.

As A, S and N walked up they looked at the queue. They felt pleased with the turn out. The freshers greeted them with subdued screams. The autographers looked straight ahead, hardly acknowledging the excited, waiting queue. However, the moment they saw P with his camera poised, they broke out into a smile; some even noticed their gait change. P took a few pics, made a show of changing lenses and then allowed the ladies to settle down in their chairs.

To ensure the queue remain orderly, K had been placed strategically near the table. K wore a sleeveless black kurta, with a red chunni tied around her waist, tied very tight…. very, very tight. Around her head was a red bandanna. One of the sleeveless arms also held a piece of wood, it was a broken leg of a chair.

There was a buzzing sound in the sky above. P's partner V had set up a drone with a video camera to film the signings. Occasionally, the petrol driven engines of the drone spluttered; however, V's deft use of his joystick shook the whole home-made contraption and cleared any fuel blockages. V was not allowed inside MB, so he monitored his positioning via visual cues provided by J, who was perched in a tree overlooking MB. Only P and V (and J) knew about J's position.

J had been in the same tree a number of times in the past. It was not always as part of P's team.

A 'Western' Encounter at Skylab

An orange summer sky glowed over Skylab. The crows were preparing to nest having fed on the last discarded scraps. Usually at this time they had the territory to themselves with no one shooing them off. The resident crows, the ones who nested in the trees in Skylab, usually ate first and nested first. Then the crows from across D lawns and sometimes as far as Nutan, drifted in to check out left over delicacies, or at mating time…socialise. It was too hot to socialise…or mate.

As for the humans, there were a few who lingered on, either lounging languidly on the sloping lawns, or having a chat with Pappu as he wound up for the night. Pappu was always cheerful, unfazed, whatever time of day it be, even when he said no to a habitual debtor.

This evening there were three 'men' leaning against Pappu's counter. They weren't even 20 yet. Boys became men very soon in this place. Two nursed their shikhanjis, one had a cheeku shake. Rolled up cigarettes dangled from the corner of their lips. It had been a long day in the workshop working on their spindles, and the grease from the lathe and the burn marks from the grinder sparks showed on their jeans.

A couple of ladies sat on the steps next to the counter drinking out of glass coke bottles. They had had a long day too. Early morning tests, struggling to find seats in some classes, bunking others, missing lunch, broke…

They were all dreading the staple Wednesday night food in their mess.

The quiet was disturbed by three speeding cycles coming to a screeching halt outside Skylab. As the dust cleared, they noticed three denim clad long haired riders throw their bikes on the ground and survey the surroundings.

The atmosphere turned electric. Even the crows stopped chirping.

The leader with a gaunt, sunken face and a mean demeanour, signalled to the other two hombres with a slight nod of the head. On cue, the two drifted to two different trees; against which they leaned. They looked causal, but their eyes were alert.

The leader marched on towards the three leaning against Pappu's counter. He stopped a few feet away from them, legs apart, ready to spring into action. He nodded at the two ladies. They understood. They got up dusted their seats with their notebooks and walked away towards the museum.

The leader stood there staring at the three. His eyes never left them. They looked at each other, trying to find support and strength as a group. The 'cheeku shake' drinker was the first one to crumble. 'It wasn't me', he said and showed the leader his spindle. The leader waved him away with a dismissive nod. Cheeku shake left his unfinished drink and scurried away. The two shikhanji drinkers were now showing their nervousness by the slow shuffle of their feet. Their hands reached out to their pockets, but they saw the sudden tensing of the leader's shoulder muscles and their hands hastily withdrew.

Without taking his eyes off them, the leader signalled one of his companions closest to the group. He sauntered down. He grabbed the cigarette from the mouth of the first shikhanji drinker and disdainfully stamped it beneath his feet. He put his hand in the pocket at the now shaking guy and removed a spindle. The other pockets were empty. He pushed him away. He scurried away as well. From a distance he, his cheeku shake companion and the ladies watched.

That left the third shikhanji drinker alone. He felt very alone. Sweat started beading on his forehead. Fear loomed on his face.

He looked at the leader and whispered: "Sorry."

Slowly, so as not to cause alarm, he reached into his pockets and removed two spindles and handed them over.

The leader stared at him for a whole minute. He selected one of the spindles and tossed the other one away.

He spat on the ground and walked to his cycle.

His two companions followed.

Compass

Yuppie had met Imli at the MB gate and they had walked away in silence.

At the bend near the temple, they stopped.

Imli stopped in the middle of the road and stood on her left leg, raising her bent right leg and resting it adjacent to the knee of the left leg.

She spread her right arm outwards and arched her left hand on her side.

She closed her eyes and rose onto the ball of her left leg.

Yuppie held her left arched hand and spun her. She came to rest with her right arm pointing towards C'Not.

Jay had hoped it would point towards Skylab. However, he graciously accepted the outcome.

They walked in silence towards C'Not.

Freshers

January, 1984.

The Gujju kid from a small town in South Central India joined BITS in the second semester, after opting out from a BE program he had joined at REC Surat in the first semester. He had made a good choice.

The kid had a soft fair pink complexion, brown hair, gold rimmed khajanchi glasses, a soft fuzzy moustache and a sky-blue jacket.

On the first day he smiled shyly at another couple of freshers; one with a wild mop of hair, cigarette on his lips: the KV guy from Chennai. The other, a somebody someone called Ajmeri.

These three from three different cultures and backgrounds bonded surprisingly well and found themselves in a wing with the infamous Biharis in the second year; the wing that would be burned down on 1 April 1985.

The scary and violent episode of the Bihari wingees room's being burnt, and D courses in the third year split this little troika, relocating them to different bhawans.

They met off and on though, the constant was the sky-blue jacket which lasted the four winters. The collar was a bit scuffed, the blue a bit faded; but it was still warm enough.

The Gujju kid was from a business family and had learnt managing finances and business from a young age. His summer vacations were spent earning a few (sizeable) rupees himself.

He also knew how to respect money. He lived frugally. He would go to the bank and withdraw five bucks at a time. He never wasted money.

He knew after graduating from BITS, he would continue managing the family business and did so successfully.

Fast forward 15 years. In Ajmeri's apartment block in Melbourne a newly married Indian couple had moved in. During introductions Ajmeri found out that the guy was a nephew of the Gujju kid.

Ajmeri got the Gujju kid's number and called him.

After a couple of minutes, he recognised his voice! There was a joyful reunion across the oceans on the phone line.

BREXIT

It had been a week since the Brexit vote.

R had hardly left his room for that week. Deeply disappointed with the vote, he had anguished and agonised over the decision.

He had replaced posters of Juhi, Kim K and Silk Smitha with David Cameron and Boris Johnson. Every now and then he would hurl a dart at their picture.

Around him lay the chassis of unfinished music systems. Usually well organised, today the room looked like a battlefield aftermath of an intense artillery war: transistors, circuit boards, knobs, soldering irons, capacitors, resistors, pieces of wire lay everywhere.

The alarm clock chimed 7.00 am. A bird tweeted persistently outside his room. His usually reserved sidee V, knocked: "utth gaya kai?" (Have you woken up?) in his Haryanvi accent. There was no response. V walked away, the slow measured pit-pat of his blue worn-out chappals beating a rhythm on the stone-floored Ashok Bhawan corridor.

Something clicked in R's mind. A tune started to form.

Rising from the bed he inserted a cassette into the nearest music system. He hit play and wound the volume knob to its full 100 W potential.

All across Ashok and RP, 'Funky Town' was heard loud and clear. To those who came to check what this early morning commotion was about, they were greeted by a vigorous, sensual, no holds barred dance by R in the dusty courtyard outside the Ashok front wing.

Michel Angelo

The Michel Angelo of the batch had obtained a new block of Carrara marble. He looked at it and saw in it potential for a masterpiece. It was perfect in colour and texture. It had no fault lines.

He wanted a model, a model that would still capture the

imagination 30 years later when he himself was 50. So, early one morning, he climbed a neem tree at the corner of the temple fence where the road from MB curved. He made himself comfortable with a six pack of beer and his favourite hat to shield himself from the sun and the early morning bird droppings.

Girl after girl left MB on their way to the Institute. In his mind's eye, he imagined them sculpted in the block of marble. Many were good, but he was looking for perfection.

'Trifles make perfection. Perfection is no trifle.'

After a few hours he gave up. He came down from the tree, walked back to his room, stripped, unsheathed his selfie stick, and took a shot of himself.

A perfect model.

Birthdays

It was his birthday.

She had first seen him in Linear Algebra class. They were usually the first ones to reserve seats in VK's class. He was always engrossed in his notes; until one day their eyes met. He had turned away shyly.

They had next met in Workshop Practice. He was nearly as bad as her in 'turning' his spindle on the lathe. As the sparks flew from the grinder, it ignited some unknown, strange, warm emotions in her. She had tried to make eye contact with him, he hid shyly behind his thick glasses.

The slow romance continued over other courses, over semesters, over chance encounters in the Audi, Oasis, and occasionally, at C'Not.

This evening she had made a quick dash to C'Not to buy soap. As she walked back to her cycle with her Hamam soap, she saw that he was being given birthday bumps by his friends. As he winced from each bump, her heart went out to him, hoping it would stop soon. Lucky he was only 20!

She shuddered at the thought of his 50th birthday!

II.

As he slept in the staff quarters, he was woken by a whirring sound in the distance, which steadily grew louder. Looking out of the window he noticed two dark shapes in the moonless night sky. As they came closer, they looked like Black Hawk stealth helicopters.

One of them hovered just outside his window and three figures winched down on a rope. Two of the figures carried assault rifles, the third clutched a package close to the bosom.

Shocked, he held his breath. There was a short sharp knock on his window. He walked up to the window as if in a daze and opened it. The two figures holding the assault rifle stepped in. Ignoring him they did a quick recce' of the house and went back to the window and nodded. The third figure stepped in and removed 'her' helmet.

As her hair cascaded from under the helmet, he recognised her. She handed him the package she was carrying. It had the seal of the United States President.

"Happy Birthday, BioS, with compliments of my husband. It has a signed copy of his latest speech."

With that, she gave him a peck on the cheek, put her helmet back on, and stepped out of the window followed by the two other figures.

In a minute or so, the whirring helicopters were disappearing over the horizon...

The dream ended a short time later.

III.

March 5; 1985, 6:00 pm

A tractor trolley entered the campus.

The trailer had 20 GKWs who sang as the tractor rumbled its way towards C'Not. At C'Not, Ratan Lal the driver stopped the tractor and opened the back gate of the trailer. Beedi at the corner of his lips, he let out the ladies one by one.

In the centre of the street the ladies formed a tight circle and slowly sang, clashing their sickles against their neighbour's sickles.

Three gentlemen who were having cheeku shakes at Kapoor's got up and marched into the centre of the circle.

The circle closed around them.

The first gentleman kicked the second one on his backside. The second gentleman kicked the third one on his backside. The third one then did the same with the first one.

They continued this until they each had received 20 kicks.

Ratan Lal then loaded his GKW's back into his tractor trailer and drove off.

The three gentlemen: U, G and L made their way back to the comfort of the moodas. It was their birthday.

IV.

September 7, 1987

The wingees were anxious. Something was in the air. Veeru was not his normal calm self.

He kept pacing the boundaries of the bhawan, looking at his watch, looking at the date. It was still 6th September. A few hours to go before midnight and then 7th September.

He shook his watch and placed it by his ear to see if it was working. There was no sound. He tried winding it up but couldn't find the wheel. He realised it wasn't a mechanical watch.

He walked up to his room and peeped through the window.

The cake was still on the table.

The 22 candles were on the cake, to be lit at midnight.

A little plaque was placed on the edge of the cake. By the moonlight the inscription was visible.

7th September.

Happy Birthday Veeru!

V.

P got up early that morning, walked out of MB in her white shorts and pink sweat top and collected some flowers from the temple lawns. She made a bouquet and put a note on it written on an IBM 1130 used punch card.

She handed it over to Giri to deliver.

20 Minutes later, Giri knocked on a door in Bhagirath. Ratan Lal came out in a daze and collected the bouquet. He gave Giri a 50 paise coin as baksheesh.

He read the note. It said: 'Happy Birthday Ratan Lal'.

Ratan Lal sighed: "Not again!"

Chumma

August, 1986

Chumma had just returned from PS1 and was determined to have an MBite 'friend'.

Those who know Chumma, will know that he was and is anything but conventional in his thinking and ideas.

On the second day of the semester, Chumma bought a notepad and 10 carbon sheets. After dinner, he lay on his tummy on his bed in Bhagirath new wing upstairs, under his rajai.

A quarter of Old Monk was parked within hand's reach, a menthol ciggie dangled from the corner of his lips. Pankaj Udhas played on the imitation Sony tape recorder.

He inserted the carbon paper between the sheets of the notepad and wrote a 'love' poem.

The words from his romantic Rajasthani heart fell delicately onto the sheets; with a difference. There was one line in Hindi, one in English. His audience spanned across the North South divide.

After the 10 copies plus original were done; he wrote a separate greeting on each one: Dear Kala, Dear Apu, Dear Shweta, Dear Vaidehi, etc.

Then he wrote the names on the envelope.

In the meantime KV guy dropped in, trying to source a spare ciggie. Chumma offered him one on condition that he would put the letters in the respective envelopes and put them in the letter box at the Post Office.

KV guy agreed.

The next few days Chumma waited with bated anticipation. He was calculating probabilities of success for the 11 letters he had sent.

Success never came.

You see KV guy was a bit hallooed that day and had inadvertently put the wrong letters in the wrong envelopes!

Chumma never found out.

He passed out from Pilani in 1987 without ever having a real MBite 'friend'.

BITS Naturist Society

The BNS (BITS Naturist Society) was having its monthly meeting on the lawns near C'Not.

Pee & Ross were the nominated ushers today. They stood on both sides of the streams handing out meeting agendas and directing members to the portable change rooms.

The stage had been set for the scheduled debate.

Hillary was practising her speech with Bill.

Gilhary was trying to squirrel/mine some dirt on Bill from his ex-intern Mon in the museum coal-mine.

The Hindi Drama Club organisers had been busy setting up the questions, the rules of engagement and organising security for what was going to be a charged debate.

The Photography Club members had taken up positions in the trees with their zoom lenses.

Thirty minutes before the debate could commence, there was a commotion outside the lawns. Chumma and N2 were leading an assorted group of disgruntled marchers.

They held banners denouncing the BNS and its charter of freedom of 'expression'.

They managed to block all access to the lawns and C'Not.

The BNS members finding their debate hijacked, marched to the Chief Warden's house and conducted a silent demonstration in their society approved 'wear'.

Meanwhile...

KV guy woke up late that afternoon. He rubbed his eyes and looked around. Seemed like he had crashed on the floor in Niger's room. He got up, looked for a cigarette, didn't find any, got out of Niger's room, stopped for a brief couple of minutes in the bogs and went to his room in Vishwakarma Bhawan.

It was a Saturday.

KV guy bathed on Saturdays.

He went to his room, picked up the Clinic Shampoo bottle *(KV guy did not believe in soap; shampoo could be used all over the body)*, changed into a cotton checked lungi/dhoti and picked up his bucket. He then realised that his immersion rod had burnt out.

So, he took his bucket, shampoo and a set of fresh dhobied clothes and decided to go to MS's room in Ram. As he left VK Bhawan, in his sleepy daze, he turned towards the IPC (Information Processing Centre where the IBM 1130 machine lived) by force of habit. KV guy spent most of his waking hours at the IPC.

When he got stares from people, he realised his folly and changed tracks towards Ram.

As he reached the corner of Sky, he found several agitators in Chumma and N2's group smoking in between their sloganeering. Finding no one familiar or generous enough to share a smoke, he thought about getting a baad-mein (pay you later) from Pappu. However, the agitators would not let him through.

Out of the corner of his eye, he could see the Hindi Drama Club members led by their Secretary 'M' in his crisp Lucknavi achkan on a hunger strike.

He made his way to Ram. As he passed the Chief Warden's house, he caught a whiff of smoke and a familiar face. Two of the BNS members had stepped out from the lawns and were having a smoke. It was his friend Niger and Niger's friend from MB, Sanu.

In his sleepy daze he asked for a cigarette. Niger said that he was running out of cigarettes himself and offered KV guy a puff.

As KV guy took a couple of puffs, his head cleared, and he realised that VK and Sanu were in their BNS approved wear!

KV guy woke up...

Nadiya ke Paar

The boy from Bareilly was excited.

His 100w PMPO system had just been delivered. There was a movie Nadiya ke Paar in the Audi tonight. His UP blood was pumping.

This was also the night he was to have his first alcoholic drink.

The wing had taken a contribution and bought a quarter bottle of Old Monk. He himself had had a late evening shower, donned his white bell-bottoms, blue janghiya and red shirt; his hair oiled with Dabur Amla Kesh tel.

They all had early dinner in the mess and returned to the wing to partake of the Old Monk and Funky Town on the 100w PMPO.

They had carried steel glasses from the mess and danced to the pulsating music.

Golcha, Camel Gait, Mallamal, Nangs, Mooon, Cookie... they danced and rocked.

His creamy cheeks became rosy with the Old Monk and the music. The boy from Bareilly had arrived.

Later they made their way to the Audi. Along with his fellow UP bhaiyyas, he felt the tugs of love and emotion and family and bhauji...

Bihar Elections

9 pm, C'Not

A circle of moodas outside Blue Moon. Some 'cats' from Delhi and surrounds sat and sipped on iced cheeku and mango shakes. They made it a point to sip through straws. They were impeccably dressed and liberally doused in cologne. The three MBites that were part of the group, wore starched kurtas and had a regal air about them.

The conversation soon wandered from Nirula's delicacies to the Ind vs SA Cricket series to Kohli's girlfriend to where to buy the cheapest Nikes to the assembly election results in Bihar.

Depending on the expertise on the subject, voices would get louder; however, the Bihari elections had the whole group very excited and predictions were made for the national elections.

Across the road at an unnamed joint, there was another circle of moodas. Here was a collection of guys (all male group) in kurtas and pyjamas/ jeans pants; the Hindi accents were Rajasthani, UP and a couple of Marathas. These guys were more in touch with the political pulse it seemed, and the Bihar election results discussion had commenced on the way to C'Not. By the time they had ordered their shikhanjis and samosas the analysis had reached a level of maturity that election pundits would have loved to emulate. They dispensed with the straws in their shikhanjis and rattled the ice in their glasses so as to get the maximum ROI.

Members of this group occasionally looked over at the group at Blue Moon; appreciating the female component of the group wistfully.

The crows in the trees above didn't seem to care about the election results.

When keys were lost...

Some of the wings in the boy's bhawans had wooden doors.

Occasionally one of the guys would come back to his room and discover he had lost his keys or left it inside the room for one of those click type locks. The only option was to get the Chowki to cut the lock and let them in.

If it was late at night, especially if one was drunk, or if Mr. Chowki was away, Ajmeri provided a small service to people who knew about it.

Ajmeri had mastered the art of banging the bottom panels in, so that they dislodged with the nails that secured them. The resident could then go in and retrieve the spare key or just go to bed and get chowki to cut the lock in the morning.

The panels were easily put back in place as they came away with the nails, without cracking or breaking up.

People thought Ajmeri could do it was because of the time

he spent in the gym; but more likely, Ajmeri had worked out the dynamics of striking at the best place to get maximum leverage and have it out in one shot. (Multiple shots would make multiple noises and attract attention.)

Now a days when Ajmeri thinks about it, he thinks this may have bordered on criminal behaviour; oh well!

Tennis

5 pm. The Pilani Tennis Courts

Pova had just finished a 1-hour practice hit out at the courts with her coach Tennis Captain Dhar.

Exhausted, she packed her racquet bag, and had a sip of Gatorade. It so happened that Tall Das had just finished 20 laps of the gym ground and they met. They had a quick chat. He offered to walk her to Meera Bhawan.

They walked past the gym on the road behind Vyas and turned towards the temple.

Tall Das carried her bag for her. She wore her frilled tennis skirt, her white Nikes, with gold trimmings and anklet socks, and a white tube top.

As they walked on the pavement, she discussed her form and her stroke play; he felt the sweet exhaustion and fatigue after a long run taking effect. As they walked occasionally, they would drift close to each other; her bare tanned shoulders grazing against his hairy arms.

They rounded the bend to MB. He handed her the racquet bag. She smiled her thanks.

He noticed Short Das at the MB gate, lounging against a tree, smoking a 'Charms'. SWilli came out of MB at a jog, stretching, flexing her quads. She wore purple shorts and a polka dot pink halter top.

Short Das stubbed out his 'Charms', gave SWilli a peck on her cheek, took hold of her racquet bag. They set out for the courts.

Tall Das followed.

It was a week before the start of the Grand Slam of Asia-Pacific: the Australian Open. This was a warm-up tournament.

II.

Fed had a long lazy shower in the Bhagirath new wing upstairs bogs.

He came out wrapped with a white towel around his waist, holding a RF soap box and a bottle of Dabur Shikakai and Amla shampoo.

He looked over the balcony across the road towards the gym.

Ivanovic had been gracefully hitting balls against the gym wall, whilst a crew of ball boys *(freshers from Shankar)* ran around collecting them.

Ivanovic had finished and was packing her kit, bent over, her back to Fed. The ball boys had handed over their collected balls to Ivanovic and had been allowed to go back to Shankar.

For a moment the poem Solitary Reaper came to Fed's mind: "Behold her, single in the field (court)..."

Still bent over, Ivanovic looked back over her shoulder and saw Fed in the balcony upstairs.

Fed felt caught out. He hurriedly put his soap and shampoo down on the balcony wall and tightened the towel around his waist.

III.

The SWilli-Pova match took place on a sunny Sunday afternoon.

Vantage points around the courts had been staked out since early that morning.

SWilli was too strong for Pova and the match was over soon with a 6-4, 6-1 result.

As SWilli leaped around the courts with joy, Pova gracefully packed her bags and threw her towels and wrist bands into the Vyas crowd, where a mini riot broke out.

Though it was the 18th straight head to head win for SWilli, the crowds were visibly disappointed.

Pova made eye contact with Tall Das; he nodded in understanding and hailed a passing rickshaw. Blowing kisses to the crowd, Pova mounted the rickshaw. Tall Das climbed in beside her and they took off to catch the 7.30 pm Haryana Roadways to Loharu.

Short Das exchanged high fives with SWilli, gave her a resounding congratulatory slap on her back and escorted her to MB where she could shower and change.

IV.

Fed had lost. He was obliterated.

Ivanovic couldn't watch the match. For long years she had watched in awe as he went from bhawan to bhawan demolishing the competition. And now this Joker was coldly, calculatedly, decisively beating her idol.

Where was the respect for history?

As this gentle giant absorbed the bruises, he rallied, won one set, and then folded up. Ivanovic couldn't look; she covered her face in her palms.

The match was soon over. Fed picked up his bags and with a defiant wave left the courts. Ivanovic hurried to wait for him at the exit.

He saw her. Their eyes met. His eyes were red; hers were teary with tenderness. She walked besides him as he trudged along.

No words were said. As they approached Bhagirath, he stopped and put his racquet bag down. He ran his fingers through his hair, still looking into the distance.

She removed a little hand towel she had in her bag, and gently wiped his forehead. Tears welled up at the corner of his eyes again. Abruptly he picked up his bags and ran up the stairs to his room.

She stood there for a few minutes, still holding the hand towel. She hung the towel on the wire fence and walked away. She turned around a few times to see whether Fed would appear in the balcony.

He didn't.

V.

1.00 am that night

A sultry, steamy night.

Fed and Ivanovic lay on their beds. They were lying on their tummies, torsos propped up on their elbows; legs bent up at the knees and folded at the ankles, swaying with gentle tension. In their dark rooms, one in Meera Bhawan, the other in Bhagirath, the screens of their smart phones in their hands cast an eerie glow.

They had been to the Saturday evening movie in the Audi with their own wingees. They had seen each other during the break and exchanged nervous looks. As the crowds filed out after the movie, he strained to look for her, unsuccessfully. She wasn't very tall.

He had come to his room, changed into his silk boxers and got a WhatsApp message: 'Goodnight', from her. He replied, 'Good Night'.

She had changed into her silky white cotton nightie. As she swayed her legs, the delicate payals on her ankles jingled softly.

She wanted to call him on 'Face time' but didn't know how he would take it. She typed in Good night again; he replied with the same message.

This went on for about half an hour.

Finally, she typed in Sweet Dreams. There was no response…
…just an emoticon of a fluffy teddy bear saying: "Zzzzzz…."

Cookie's Saturday morning

In 219 Bhagirath, Cookie woke up on Saturday morning. He got up from his bed, stretched, yawned, tightened his pyjama strings and reached for his glasses.

He needed to go to the loo and looked for a newspaper. He took out the sports page, put it under his armpit, collected his soap dish and made his way to the bogs.

He returned after an hour, pleasantly relieved by the exercise/activity; not so happy about the write up in the paper about the cricket umpiring.

Before going for breakfast, he sat down on the armchair outside R's room and polished his new Kolhapuris. R's own Kolhapuris were there as well, soggy and wrecked. Cookie always felt R was a bit...a bit of a Camel Gait, really.

M1, M2, Nan**, and Dukki had woken as well.

They all went together to the mess for Thanksgiving Day Breakfast.

VM's empty room

(This was written when my close friend Cookie passed away; taken by cancer)

Gupta woke up early this morning. There was a stillness in the air. He opened his door. There was a newly polished pair of Kolhapuris outside his door.

He looked at his sidee's room. The door was open.

His sidee was an early riser; Gupta wasn't surprised. He walked over and peeped in.

The room was empty.

The mattress was gone from the bed. The bed lay there stark in its rough wooden nakedness.

The desk was empty too, missing the pile of textbooks and notebooks.

The posters from the walls had been neatly removed, barely leaving any marks.

The brown paper covering the glass windowpanes had gone as well, making the room look brighter than it ever had.

The curtain covering the shelves had gone too, so had the shelf paper liners.

The fan on the ceiling whirred slightly, propelled by an invisible breeze.

The back windows had been left open. On a branch on a neem tree outside, sat a lone bird, very quiet, very still.

Jimmy and Moody walked in.

They watched the emptiness, felt the quiet; yet their ears were full of the laughter, the arguments about cricket; the discussions on the right way to cook rajma that had filled this room.

Jimmy being the tallest, saw something left behind in one of the top shelves.

There were the three tennis balls, including the prized one. He took them down. The three of them walked down to the gym.

They didn't look at each other. They feared the others would see their eyes welling up with tears.

They stopped near the tennis courts and one by one tossed the tennis balls as far as they could. The balls swung and bounced a few times. Far away, they came to a rest in the green grass, until they could be seen no more….

Of Bulls and Bull Workers

A bull had strayed into MB.

It was early morning. The MB gates were not guarded that well at that time. The bull strolled around to the back of the bhawan, nibbling on the virgin, verdant grass. He went unnoticed for a long time, until a late riser on the ground floor opened her back window to come face to face with this horned beast licking his lips after a satisfying breakfast. His tongue extended through the window grill and swallowed her Report Writing notes.

Hearing her screams, her wingees came to her help. Whilst the leaders and politically minded expressed their displeasure at the chowki (security guard) and went to upbraid him, a couple of others snatched brooms and tried to poke the bull in his snout. He left his Report Writing delicacy and snatched the brooms from their hands, swallowed half of them and spat out the rest on the other side.

An ingenious mind went to the room above the offending bull and poured a bucket of water from the window. The bull didn't seem to mind, the water drove away the flies that were bothering him and also cooled him down. He lapped at the puddle formed below and turned his attention back to the window.

Meanwhile, behind the bull a group was gathering dressed in nighties, salwars, half sarees, etc, with ideas being shared in Telegu, Hindi, Tamil, even the soft gentle tones of Bengali.

The bull turned to look at them and the group took a step back.

'X' from the 83 batch had just finished her morning Bull Worker routine and stepped out to see what the commotion was about.

Sweating in pink and white leotards, she marched to the bull with her Bull Worker. Some smarty found it funny: "Prodding a bull with a Bull Worker. Ha ha ha!" No one else found it amusing.

The bull wasn't impressed. He snorted at her. Glistening with sweat, she approached him on her toes, knees bent and primed, ready to back out and run if needed. The group behind her cheered her on. The motherly types watching from upstairs shrieked caution. The bull ignored her and started moving on towards the back wall, spotting some more green grass. The group behind him dispersed, in various directions. Someone, in an oversize nightie, tripped and fell. Someone else pulled her back on to her feet.

The bull started eating the grass again. By this time the warden and some mess servants had arrived. 'X' tried to launch an attack on the bull by hitting it on its haunches with her Bull Worker. The bull swung his tail as a warning, and she withdrew.

One of the mess servants approached 'X' and asked that the bull be left to him. 'X' said that she was more than capable of handling him. The mess guy then whispered something in her ear. She looked at the bull with new eyes, coloured up, let out a gasp and immediately withdrew.

The mess guy slowly approached the bull, caught its tail, shouted a few earthy exhortations and had the bull moving towards the gates and out.

The excitement died down. The leaders were still berating the chowki.

After the movie

Imli walked her bicycle to the Audi steps. She climbed the second step and mounted the cycle. Yuppie still trying to make up with her after their stoush, held the carrier behind the cycle. Imli pushed off. Yuppie ran behind the cycle. Once the cycle had stabilised, he jumped and sat on the carrier.

The cycle wobbled for a bit. Imli let out an audible "Hmph"...and cycled on...

Imli's cycle with Yuppie on the carrier gathered speed. She loved the curved road in front of the Audi where she could bend her right shoulder and incline the cycle at an angle of 23.5 degrees. This connected her inner self with the principal alignments of the universe.

However, it was tough for Yuppie on the carrier who hung on for dear life; left hand cradling Imli's purse, right hand trying to find a grip under her seat between the springs. The absence of cushioning on the cycle carrier made matters worse.

The sugar from the M&Ms Imli had consumed during the movie had created new energy in her. The thigh muscles pumped the pedals with Olympian vigour. Her agility with the handle in the semi darkness, weaving through relaxed pedestrians was a sight to behold. Yuppie was enjoying the ride. This is why she fascinated him.

She suddenly had to slam her brakes, Vikramsinh dressed in his All England Tennis Club (Wimbledon) purple coat and whites was leisurely walking in the centre of the street eating his strawberries and cream.

Besides him Jhumla was busy on his calculator. Mangey was jotting down a nazm he had just composed on his palm with a pen. KV guy was making a 'cigarette'.

Imli rang her cycle bell furiously. Yuppie tried to look beyond her sweating back, to see what the hold-up was.

II.

Ratan Lal appeared from the bushes, wiping his hands. He saw the scene, spoke to the pedestrians and created space for her bike to move.

She nodded to Ratan Lal as she passed him. Yuppie smiled at him and tossed him an M&M.

Imli had to come to a halt again, rather suddenly. Yuppie

winced again as he collided with her back. He had an idea about inventing cycle helmets. He adjusted his glasses and waited. Imli meanwhile stood legs astride the ladies' cycle.

At the intersection of Budh and Ram, there was a large agitated gathering. In the fading glow of the streetlight, the shadowy figures were scurrying frantically. She heard the word 'accident' multiple times. She tried walking her cycle past the mob, but it was difficult to manoeuvre, especially since Yuppie was still sitting on the carrier, gently gazing at Ratan Lal walking behind them. She tilted her bike at 30 degrees, which moved Yuppie's centre of gravity past the median and he landed awkwardly on his feet. Ratan Lal helped him stand up straight and was rewarded with another M&M for his efforts.

Imli moved her cycle on the kerb to get a better view of the accident. Ali was running up from Budh having 'borrowed' a chair for the accident victim Feroze.

There was a girl in there as well, attending to Feroze. She was wiping something off Feroze's shoulder with the corner of her chunni.

Feroze always wore a sherwani for movies in the Audi. It was usually a black one for a Hindi movie and a white one with gold zari for English movies. For the odd Dubba movies he went to, he wore a Tommy Hilfiger jacket.

It became clear that a stupid crow had deposited a splat on Feroze's black sherwani.

Imli rang her bell furiously, but was immediately hushed by the 'Little Flower' alumni association.

Tapsy, meanwhile had made his way to the front wing upstairs and was focussing his binoculars on Katy.

Imli decided to take a detour. She wheeled her cycle around, stood on the kerb, mounted it and took off. Yuppie ran behind, Imli's handbag in one hand and got back onto the carrier.

III.

After all the roller coaster emotions of the movie and the 'Little Flower' event; Imli decided to take a longer, more scenic route back, at a more leisurely pace. She took her angry pulsing finger off the cycle bell and eased the rpm on the cycle pedals. Most of the crowds had cleared off the streets. There was a stillness in the air. Her planned route was past VK, RP, the Bank, around the front of RP, Ashok, heading past the staff quarters towards C'Not.

Yuppie sat peacefully, unruffled, perched trustingly on the carrier. He was enjoying the gentler pace, and his mind drifted to happier times when he had first met Imli.

A matter of keys

A certain batchmate after a few beverages, went to the Audi for a movie and promptly fell asleep.

As the snoring was not palatable to his fellow audience, during the break they walked him to the exit door and he wandered back to his bhawan.

He walked up to room 279 and tried his key in the lock. It didn't work. He then proceeded to kick the panels of the wooden door and crawled into the room. After fixing the panels back in, he collapsed into bed and resumed his snoring stupor.

He was woken up by a scream and a half-undressed male.

The 'snorer' had wandered into 279, Shankar instead of 279, Vyas!

Dawn raid

Short, fair and curly-haired (SFCH) dada's room (115 Ashok) had been raided in the early morning, around 7:00 am by the Chowki.

The previous night, SFCH dada had crashed in his friend P Rao's room. He wasn't there when the room was raided.

The chowki prepared a list of liquor bottles totalling 16 litres found in SFCH Dada's room. This included:

Old Monk: 5 litres
Bagpiper Gold: 4 litres
Bagpiper: 3 litres
McDowell's No 1: 2 litres
Bottles without labels with orange-ish alcohol: 2 litres

The RPA veg mess-sec returned to his room (108 Ashok) at 8.00 am after a morning gym session and having gulped 6 raw eggs in the mess.

He was told about the raid in his wingee's room and felt that his room had also been entered (a few magazines had been disturbed!)

He was heard saying that the SMC co-ordinator was a coward and a psychopath!

GVG at the pool

Swimming his fourth straight lap in the swimming pool, GVG suddenly had a feeling of being a bit free and gay.

From the sidelines he saw Paulda, the swimming coach frantically trying to get his attention.

GVG looked at the other end of the pool where Paulda was pointing and spotted his swimming trunks drifting lazily in the water.

GVG had had a wardrobe malfunction...

Lights Out

Tall Dutta, Shams and Ajmeri returned to their wing in Ashok from the gym at about 8 pm. Tall Dutta and Ajmeri were then in the ground floor new wing opposite the gym grounds. Shams was a fresher and decided to tag along because he wanted to go to the loo, and Ashok was nearer than his own bhawan.

Shams was about 6'5'' and went on to become weightlifting captain after two 83 batchers (Ajmeri and Jimmy) had had a go.

Ajmeri went to his room, changed to a towel wrapped around him, to head for a shower. Shams went to Tall Dutta's room; stripped to his jocks, borrowed his soap case and started his march to the bogs.

Just then the lights went off. It happened to be a moonless night. It became pitch dark. Ajmeri had never experienced such darkness. Pilani, at that time didn't have any vehicular traffic to speak of, and the whole campus was dark. There was zero visibility.

As the three stood where they were, they heard a feminine cry from the road saying "Help!"

Shams and Ajmeri knowing that they were in a state of partial undress, weighed up whether they should find their way to their rooms and get some clothes on in the dark, or find out who needed help and why. There was another 'Help' cry. Chivalry prevailed and they made their way in the dark towards the road trying not to trip over anything. The girls heard them coming and they heard a voice saying: "Thank You." "We are scared of this darkness; can you stay with us until the lights come back on?" They said sure, but a million thoughts were racing through their minds. Ajmeri was stinking of sweat after 3 hours in the gym, but Shams was in a worse state. Ajmeri could make out by his shuffling that he was desperate to go the loo. Also, he was conscious of being attired only in his jocks.

A voice again came from one of the girls; "Hi. I am Selma and with me is… we were on our way back from Nutan." Shams and Ajmeri said "Hi", and in their continuing embarrassment forgot to give their names or contribute to any of the small talk.

5 minutes later the lights came on. The scene: Selma and this other girl on the side of the road clinging to their bikes, within 3 feet of two sweaty guys, one in his jocks with a soap case, and the other trying to hold on to his towel in the breeze. One of the girls almost screamed. They were embarrassed and rode off into the night.

Shams dashed to the bogs. Ajmeri went and told the rest of the wingees that he had met Selma!

Mother

108, Ashok. 11:00 pm

He lay on his bed thinking of his mother.

He had last seen her in January. He remembered that day. She had woken up early that morning and made his favourite paranthas with eggs. The tea had been special too, with cardamom and ginger.

All morning she had fussed around, making sure he had packed everything. Every half hour she would admonish him lovingly: "You should write more often;" " Eat well, see how thin you were when you came home on vacation."

Mid-morning, she had quietly passed him an envelope with some secret money: "Don't tell dad..."

Lunch had been a slow elaborate affair: fresh steamed rice, Goan fish curry, prawn chilli-fry: "You won't get this in Pilani."

As he had left in the auto for the bus stand, she tried not to make eye contact. He knew after he had gone, she would have a silent cry.

He lay there on his bed. He would see her in another week at end of the semester. Tears welled up in his eyes.

He missed her.

He loved her...he didn't tell her that often enough...

II.

Sometime in the next semester...

He had mail. Unlike the usual blue inland letters, this time it was a yellow postal envelope.

It was addressed to him in the familiar neat handwriting of his mother. It evoked a different emotion than his dad's handwriting. He knew there'd be words of love, worry about his health and food and sleep. The handwriting would go just a bit astray when she got emotional and teary eyed. Reading it hundreds of kilometres away on an impersonal sheet of folded paper, the emotion would carry to him. More than the words, the inflection in the handwriting communicated love.

He always read his mum's letters when he was alone. He kept them and read them again and again.

When he was sick or lonely or had done badly in a test he went back to her letters.

He opened this one today. It was two pages.

Besides the usual news of his siblings and the grumble about the maids and the weather and her workload as a school teacher; she had put in a photocopy of certificate she had received for 25 years as a teacher with a photo of the presentation. He could almost smell the flowers she held, hear the soft folds of her sari rustle, feel her gentle loving hands massaging his brow...

Weekend at Meera Bhawan

She woke up early one spring morning to the cacophony of bird calls.

She had left her window open in the night. The first rays of the sun cast a warmth on her face and annoyed her sleepy eyes.

She woke up, stretched and walked out to the balcony. Everyone else seemed to be still asleep on this Sunday morning. Even the 'traffic' moving outside MB was missing.

She went back to her room, closed her window, drew the curtains, lay down, pulled the bed sheet over herself and went back to sleep.

A familiar sound woke her up.

Her hungover sidee was talking in her sleep, yet again: "Vivek, Rajneesh, Viren, Jaya, Naru, Srini, Srinu, Ramesh, Rakesh, Sexy, Bhattu, Malhu, Sai, Panju, Nangu, Raj, Venky, Giri, Chiru, Syed, Jolly, Taps, Arvind...." It went on and on...

She leaned down from her bed and threw a shoe at her sidee's wall.

The litany stopped...

...there was a pause.

Then a deep, passionate "Sanjay."

Then silence...

She went back to sleep.

II.

There was a knock on her door. Nina wanted to borrow her broom.

She threw the other shoe at the door. Nina walked away.

Someone passing by her door sneezed.

It was quite a distinct sneeze. It was Kala. The sneeze was loud; loud not only in decibel count, but also tended to send a ripple of shockwaves, which would rattle loose windowpanes.

When she sneezed in a corridor, some people believed they heard echoes for some time.

She had no more shoes left to throw.

When she awoke, the sun was high in the sky. The birds were having their afternoon slumber. She felt hungry. She got off her bed and with half-closed, sleepy eyes, felt around for her shoes.

They weren't there.

She tucked her 'Go Pro camera' around her neck and took a barefoot 'hike' to the mess...humming…

III.

Meanwhile in the upstairs back wing in MB, most people followed their Sunday morning routine.

Apu's sidee Penaaz liked sleeping on the floor, so her wooden bed was in the passageway used as a communal chaupal (meeting place).

Today Penaaz was perched on the bed in the mid-morning sun, with Apu leaning against her. Penaaz was grooming, oiling and plaiting Apu's hair. Later they would swap places. They had been doing this for three sems now and no one bothered anymore. Sometimes, when they had a tiff, they did it in silence. While they discussed Sanjay and other people, Apu carefully made a garland of some jasmine buds she had plucked that morning. The smell was refreshingly pleasant. Kala sat at the other corner of the bed. Kala was doing her nails and there was a strong smell of nail polish remover. Kala did not contribute to the conversation, but rumour had it she 'listened'.

Meanwhile, Sanjay was also following his Sunday morning routine. He usually slept in until lunch…in the buff.

The KV guy

Saturday afternoons the KV guy had his weekly bath.

At this time the bogs were usually empty, and he could sing his Tamil-Eagles fusion with 'gay' abandon whilst his body renewed its acquaintance with water.

The KV guy believed in minimalist living. He bought a bottle of Clinic Plus shampoo at the beginning of the sem. He used the shampoo as soap as well.

The spare lungi doubled/tripled up as a towel and bedsheet.

So this Saturday, as usual he showered, scrubbed, washed, changed, ran a pink comb through his mop and started his march from Shankar to Ram, where Niger and MS waited.

As he went round the bend on the road towards Ram a tinkling of bells alerted him to a swarm of MBites on a random joy ride on their ladies bikes.

With this shock of young femininity overwhelming him, KV Guy felt something strange happening inside him; strange enough that he quickly turned back and went back to his room.

Something was wrong.

He went into his room, ignored his sidee's snide remark of him looking 'hot'; and closed his door.

He unzipped and sure enough discovered what was wrong.

He had forgotten to put on a critical item of clothing...

Another Day...

It was KV Guy's first trip to MB.

He had met her at the IPC and helped carry her printouts to her cycle. He had even put the printout bundle in her cycle carrier, injuring his finger as he put it under the spring-loaded clasp. Seeing the drop of red Tamilian blood, she had wiped it off with her yellow Telegu Desam handkerchief, and then tied it on his finger.

That physical contact sent two twenty year old hearts in a spin of unexplored romance and she shyly invited him to call on her at MB next day.

He had woken early, washed his mop with the remnants of the Clinic Plus, wiped it with a fresh dhoti, and climbed on a chair to dry his hair under the ceiling fan.

He donned his acid wash bell bot jeans, wore a crisp white shirt, folded the sleeves twice, just right, wound his HMT Kohinoor watch and unbuttoned the top two buttons in his shirt to expose the two hair on his chest.

By habit he slipped on his chappals, headed to MS's room in Ram to dab on a splash of Old Spice.

On the way his chappal strap came off and he sat on the side of the road to readjust the safety pin that held the strap in place.

He heard a twinkling of bells as a group of chlorine soaked MBites rode on their way back from the swimming pool.

He decided to sit there for some time...

Another time...

One evening in '87 a few guys were lying on the mandir lawns in the late evening, killing time before the mess opened for dinner, enjoying the cool breeze, watching the birds circling in the clear blue sky and discussing random stuff...as you do.

KV Guy who was prone to having quite a vivid imagination, asked the group about the probability of one of the circling bird's dropping falling into his mouth. Everyone ignored him, but KV Guy kept his mouth open and sure enough a splat landed in his mouth within a minute. The group ran for cover as he furiously spat out the stuff.

Ajmeri was with the KV Guy that day. He spoke to him briefly after 25 years. KV Guy lives in the Bay Area. He has a thick American accent. It is believed it is because he lives in the States.

Saturday night

On the way back from the Audi, after watching Blue Lagoon, Camel Gait and KV Guy walk back to Bhagirath, sharing a cigarette.

No talk.

Lost in their thoughts.

The embers of the diminishing cigarette connecting them in silence.

Steady beat of KV Guy's Bata chappals and Camel Gait's Kolhapuris.

Camel Gait wondering where he could get a poster of Brooke Shields.

KV Guy wondering where he would sleep tonight...

...definitely not in Camel Gait's room

Entrepreneur

It was the final semester before PS 2 and Bhila was thinking of job opportunities.

So far, the campus interviews hadn't been very promising. He had two offers from some vague companies and nearly accepted them, even though they didn't pay much.

One day he had struck up a conversation with his dhobi in Bhagirath and found out that the dhobi's son was doing quite well as a rickshaw puller.

Bhila figured out that with his marketing skills learnt through the management elective he had done and sales skills from the coke/special stuff stand he had run at Oasis and his knowledge of the campus traffic and hot spots for customer demand: he could double the income he earned from the two offers.

So, next day he hired a rickshaw for a day to test his 'theory'. He rode early morning to Nutan bus-stand and promptly got 'hired' to 'cart' a local family that had arrived post a wedding in Jhunjhunu.

The family consisted of a husband, a wife, four kids, five sacks and a goat and a bag of goat feed.

The rest is history.

Pyjama Debate

It may not be the most cultured or academic or proper topic, but the fact is, it happened and some of the most brilliant minds of the 83 batch were involved. So here goes...

Well the discussion topic was when one went to the bogs whether the whole pyjama came off or was it just folded to the knees. (those days these were Indian style WCs, so it made a difference).

After some arguments, the matter was put to vote. Surprisingly, the votes were very near equal.

The reasons each side provided trying to convince the others that their method was better were too graphic.

Obviously the lungiwallahs were excluded from the polls and had a few digs at the crazy north Indians.

At that time in the corridors of the bhawans, there was no topic beyond the realms of discussion and heated arguments.

C'Not

Bablu sat alone on a mooda in a corner of C'Not, waiting for her. He looked at his watch every two minutes.

He was trying to consume his shikhanji as slowly as possible. Even the ice had melted in the shikhanji. All that was left was a few drops with two surviving lime seeds.

Every time a cycle turned up the road into the C'Not road, he looked anxiously. It wasn't her.

He was tempted to light up a cigarette, but after the tantrum she had thrown the last time, he didn't dare.

In order to ease his nerves, he started singing the old Hindi song: Merey sapnon ki rani, kab aayegi tu? (My dream girl, when will you come?)

Just then SRK spotted Bablu sitting alone. He lowered himself into the mooda opposite Bablu. Bablu had been keeping the mooda for her. SRK proceeded to drink up the remaining dregs of the shikhanji and asked Bablu: "Cigarette hai kya?" (Do you have a cigarette?).

She didn't come that day.

Rakhi

10.30 pm

After the movie the two of them walked her to MB. They discussed the movie, the actors, the songs.

Bablu read Stardust regularly and displayed his knowledge

about the actors, their affairs and the prices they charged per movie proudly.

Saba was quiet. His eyes were on her profile, speculating. At the MB gate, they said bye.

She held onto Bablu's hand. He looked at her slightly embarrassed. From her little purse, she removed a rakhi and tied it on his wrist. Bablu borrowed a fiver from Saba and gave it to her.

Saba waited for his turn. It didn't happen.

She shut her purse, pinched him suggestively on his palm, winked and ran into the gates.

Saba slowly raised his palm to his lips, kissed it and blew towards where she had run.

Audi trip with the classy ones

Ajmeri joined Pilani in the second semester.

His classmate from school, MP, had joined in the first semester. It took Ajmeri two weeks to find MP as the guys in Shankar-Vyas supposedly didn't know their batch mates in Ram Budh where MP lived.

However, he did finally make contact,and MP asked Ajmeri to join his wingees for a movie at the Audi one Saturday.

By this time, Ajmeri had been through a few ragging episodes mainly by '83 batch first semmers. When he went to MP's wing, this group of wingees were different.

They were all getting 'ready' to go to the Audi; taking special care to dress neatly, hair done, shoes polished etc. It was an occasion. They spoke a strange version of Hindi. Having grown up in Rajasthan, this was Ajmeri's first exposure to Hyderabadi Hindi/Urdu. There was a strong waft of cologne/ ittar in the air as well!

Ajmeri's initiation/ragging exercise was to remove his coat and put it back on 'elegantly'. Try it; it's not that easy, if one is wearing a turtleneck at the same time.

One of them even checked under Ajmeri's turtleneck collar to see if he was wearing a shirt and whether it was clean.

He passed all the tests and was allowed to accompany them to the movie.

That was the last time he accompanied them, maybe because of his lack of class and the peer pressure to dress up.

It was easier with the Biharis with their gamchas and pyjamas.

Ice Bucket Challenge

January 30, 1987

7:00 am

Jay has woken up early. He doesn't want his wingees to know that today is the day that he will prove it to them: He can take up the challenge!

3 years they've riled him. Today, it will all change.

He dresses up, locks his door and heads out. He goes past the gym. There is some loser working out on a cold Saturday morning by himself. He passes behind the SV mess. The mess servants are busy getting breakfast ready. A plume of smoke rises from the mess chimney.

He turns around Vyas and goes past the temple. Some freshers are at the temple offering early morning prayers. He did that in his first year too.

He is on his final leg. The heart beats faster. The fog is heavy around the bend to Meera Bhawan. The tree branches are quiet. The birds are still asleep.

He approaches the MB gates. The chowki asks him what he wants.

He says: "Can you call P from room 2—?"

The chowki says it's too early. Jay says it is urgent. Chowki sizes him up. Jay looks innocent and sincere.

He announces Jay. Jay waits.

She is taking her own time. There are a couple of girls going to the temple. They look at him shyly. He looks away. Finally, ten minutes later P arrives. She is still half asleep. She asks him what he wants?

He says: "Can I borrow a bucket?"

She says: "What?"
He says, he needs to borrow a bucket.
She asks: "What for?"
He says: "For the Ice Bucket Challenge."

Skylab

His pulse started racing each time he entered the Skylab lawns.

It raced for a few reasons. One, there were girls. He hadn't spoken to one in his three semesters so far. He had spoken about them. He had heard stories about them. He had fantasised about them. To him they were another species. There were guys (people called them 'cats') who hung around with the girls. They laughed and joked and walked around with that air...the 'air'. They knew and spoke to and socialised with that special species, the girl!

The other reason was the money. He could possibly afford a chai; he didn't need one. It just felt great to stand at Pappu's counter and order something. It was a sense of power, of belonging; although, each time he spent he thought of his bank account, how his parents struggled to pay for his expenses.

He would look for his friends hanging out at Sky. A group like him in some ways. A group that hadn't found its way to talk to girls. A group different in some ways; some of them had money. The bond of not knowing how to socialise with girls was the bond that held them together.

They spoke, they joked; yet their eyes were on the girls and the privileged guys who were with them.

They dressed, they groomed, they did the best they could, but then they returned to their bhawans, their messes, their late night hangouts at Nutan or late night canteens or their own rooms, with their text books and notebooks and Debs.

Days passed.

He lived on, on gossip, on fantasies, on dreams…

The Linear Algebra class monitor

The Prof had been called to an urgent meeting with the Director, so he had to leave his class in a hurry.

He didn't like to leave his class midway, given the amount of prep he put into it. It was also great exercise for him as he dashed from one end of the blackboard to the other at this large lecture theatre, linking scenarios together and proving his 'theories'.

The Prof. enjoyed the engagement his pupils had; as a hundred heads followed his every movement, not unlike spectators at a tennis game.

From his research on his students, he knew he had a qualified 'monitor' in the class. He called AB to look after the class whilst he was away.

AB took his position at the head of the class, pacing in the Prof's illustrious footsteps. He studiously avoided looking at the board, keeping his attention on the pupils.

AB had Engineering Graphics class next; his drafter hung from his belt like a Colt 45.

C and her ghotu friends got into a huddle to discuss what the Prof had taught so far. The buzz radiated waves which reached D M and his friends who sat a few rows behind. D M was one who staked seats for himself and his friends from Kurnool, making sure he got there an hour before the class. He so wanted to hear what the MB ghotu group were discussing, but he was shy.

Also interested in the MB ghotu group were S and his friends. They had long given up hope of anything but a 'C' in Linear Algebra. They were interested in the MB ghotu group for different reasons than D M. The reasons weren't academic at all.

They S group loudly discussed evening plans, their encounters at Nirula's in the last summer break, the latest movie starring Zeenie, etc.

AB tried to quieten them with his looks, but they wouldn't heed him. He picked up a piece of chalk and threw it Bruce Lee style. It whistled past S's ears, crashed into the wall behind, shattered and sprayed the group with white powder. S cleaned the powder off his glasses and looked at AB with new respect.

SP sitting by the window, looked into the windowpane at his own reflection, trying to block his moustache with a finger, arguing with himself: to keep a moustache or not.

The Prof returned to the class. AB walked back to his desk, unsheathed his drafter and laid it on the desk.

The MB ghotu group disbanded.

Normal programming resumed. 27 years later AB would go on to shepherd one of the batch social media groups.

Uber

Uber was trialling a driverless rickshaw in the Vidya Vihar campus.

They decided to do the trial at night. Though a note was pinned in each mess informing of the trial; some people missed it.

The rickshaw entered the campus at 10.30 pm. Uber had placed two life like dummies in the seat: 1 male and 1 female, modelled on a couple from the 83 batch.

As the rickshaw passed the swimming pool, Girdhari and his wingees on their way to Nutan respectfully made way. They then had an argument about who the couple were.

Jonty ran back along the sidewalk towards Ashok to verify.

Jimmy was returning from a late evening rendezvous at the Gliding Club and cycling with testosterone infused passion towards Ashok. He nearly ran into the Uber rickshaw. He screeched to a halt and muttered choice Haryanvi epithets, before noticing the 'lady' in the back seat and tipping his hat to her.

Neither Jimmy, nor Girdhari, nor Jonty noticed the rickshaw was driverless. They were all distracted by the 'lady'.

…..............

As the rickshaw neared the temple, A, B and C who were returning to MB noticed the rickshaw and the couple. They spoke in whispers about the 'couple'. They didn't notice the lack of the driver either.

Lying in the temple lawns, KV guy 'woke' up to go to a friend's room for the night. He was tired/dazed/hallooed and thought he'd get a free ride in the rickshaw. He hailed the rickshaw and noticed it was driverless.

He rubbed his eyes and blinked a few times trying to focus. The rickshaw had passed from view.

In the dark, A, B and C bumped into KV. All four screamed.

Meanwhile...

Sitting atop the clock tower with night vision binoculars and the controls to the rickshaw was Bubba bhai.

The night vision glasses also displayed images from the geospatial cameras mounted in four places around the rickshaw.

He filmed the precise turn of events that caused the screams.

All this time his lady friend perched next to him on the clock tower fed him peanuts.

"Madam, your tail is in my lap"

One summer night in '87 a group of wingees was at the Audi watching a rather sedate romantic movie.

They had done their due diligence with the prep. They'd been to the mess early for dinner and paid appropriate respects to Ms Old Monk and Gold Flake; been in early in the Audi and occupied seats somewhere on the ground floor. All very normal really.

As the Audi started filling in, there was a group of MBites who came in and occupied the row in front of the wingees. Group of well-behaved ladies in their first year from Andhra. They giggled away quite excited with their little jokes in Telegu. Quite normal really.

It was a sedate movie as mentioned before; no loud comments, chair smashing or cries of "Repeat, Narang-ji." (Narang-ji was the projectionist.)

Sometime into the movie, the wingee sitting next to Tall Dutta felt him squirming in his seat. The wingee wondered if it was Ms Old Monk or a toilet call. He asked him and Tall Dutta pointed to the girl seated on the chair in front of him. The wingee could see nothing out of the ordinary about her, but maybe Tall Dutta was feeling something special, so he let him be. It was a romantic movie after all.

During the interval, Tall Dutta leaned forward, tapped the girl on her shoulder and said: "Madam, your tail is in my lap." It was her hair which was tickling his short-exposed thighs all this time.

The hair was instantly withdrawn and parked over the front of the girl's 'parachute'.

Tall Dutta was comfortable after that.

Sunday languid lazy arvos

It was one of those January Sunday afternoons.
Bhagirath Bhawan
After washing clothes, cleaning the room, shower and a meal of pulao, mutter-paneer and raita followed by a slice of cassata ice-cream and a chotta (small) Gold Flake or Wills Navy cut, one would go to the room, put the fan on full-speed and take a nap…zzzzzz…

Sometimes the zzzzz... was disturbed by one of Bubba's 100 watts music system customers. That's when one would come out of the room clutching a hastily wrapped towel around one's waist, using an array of colourful multi-lingual vocab one had picked up over the years. Sometimes it worked, sometimes it didn't. Usually a bribe of a Debonair would quieten the music system owner.

Meera Bhawan
The day started off cold. The room heater stayed on until 8:00am. Breakfast optional. Languid lunch and then the warm afternoons.

Even the boys stayed away Sunday afternoons; except the odd despo. Romance took a break.

The tests hadn't commenced yet. The second semmer freshers were no longer a novelty.

The ladies relaxed in the sun. Nails got done, letters written, rooms organised.

Bit of gossip, bit of childish play, a couple of harmless pranks.

Even the birds in the neem trees softened their chirping.

MB was in sublime inertia.

Raddiwala at Bhagirath

It was a Sunday afternoon towards the end of term and the raddiwala (they bought old newspapers, bottles etc.) was visiting the Bhagirath upstairs p wing.

It had been a busy morning for the wing as they swept their rooms, changed sheets, wrote letters, reorganised posters on the walls.

The raddiwala's coming to the wing was an occasion. Here was an opportunity to get some extra money; maybe pay off debts to Nagar-ji, Pappu, the cigarette selling mess servant...

At the start of the semester when newspaper orders had been placed, groups of two or three had decided to 'share' newspapers and some magazines, as per their taste. As the semester went by, living in close proximity sometimes brought friction in relationships and therefore affected these partnerships. It was amusing then when they approached the raddiwala to bargain, using him as a mediator.

Twelve guys crowded around the raddiwala. The Management guys tried to take over the bargaining. When economic principles didn't work; they called in the sole C group guy to use stand-over tactics. However, the raddiwala was made of tougher material having been through this multiple times.

The Mechanical guys tried to examine the scales (taraazu). The lever principles, the fulcrum, the manipulation by the little finger created some discussion. The raddiwala resigned himself to this seemingly useless chatter, lit himself a beedi and started flipping through a copy of the Illustrated Weekly. The 'With Malice towards one and all' page with the portly surd attracted his attention. The' taraazu' was 'fixed'. The raddiwala had a quiet sneer, he knew more tricks than these engineers in training could dream of.

The weighing commenced. Twelve pair of eyes watched with bated breath. The EEE guy had his revered FX-82 out of its pouch adding up the totals, whilst the raddiwala kept a mental tally. As the weighing of the first lot neared completion, the FX-82 battery ran out. They asked the raddiwala to weigh it again. He said he already had kept tally. Those waiting to get their loads weighed sided with the raddiwala. He reached into his kurta pocket and paid out the first customers. They walked off.

And so, it went on. Occasionally the mech guys would shout accusing the raddiwala of sleight of hand. He would weigh it again with the same result.

After the newspapers were done, the beer bottles and Old Monk bottles came out. The economics of the glassware was different. The beer bottles were sold by number; the Old Monk bottles, despite their better 'looks' were sold by weight. The Management guys explained that this was because the beer bottles were reusable.

All through this the raddiwala kept mumbling about how he was being cheated, how low his margins were, etc.

Then it was all over. The fans in the rooms were put on top speed, doors closed, people snuggled under the sheets and dozed off.

The raddiwala arranged his stuff and walked down the deserted corridor to the stairs.

Another day...

Movie night before the test

He had decided to miss the movie in the Auditorium.

With a makeup on Monday, and bad marks in the first two tests, this was a critical test.

After dinner, almost everyone had gone for the movie. Some wanted good seats, so they had an early dinner and left straight from the mess. Being in the upstairs back wing, he could hear whole wings passing by noisily. Stragglers ran to catch up with their friends. There was a regular pounding on the stairs. He had changed into his favourite lungi, switched on the table lamp on the desk, got his notes out, opened the textbook, looked at the Favre-Leuba alarm clock on his desk.

Tick-Tock it went…

The ceiling fan was on low speed. Even then it managed to rustle the pages of his notebook. It was a still night outside, and as the bhawan was nearly deserted, he opened his front door and the window.

An inland letter from his little sister back home had arrived yesterday. He had read it twice already. He opened it again and read it. She had beautiful handwriting. He could feel her excitement and bubbly nature, as her letter randomly shifted between describing her role in the school concert, the class picnic she had been to, the neighbour's new dog (with a drawing of the dog), the decorations on their street for the temple festival that was coming up. He missed his sister. His eyes welled up.

He went to the corridor and looked out. A few rooms still had their lights on. Some guys hadn't joined the movie club. Others had just left their lights on; they always left their lights on. The naked bulbs in the corridor cast a dull glow. The sudden silence after all the noise of people going to the Audi was deafening.

He went to the bogs, took a leak, washed his hands and strolled back to his room.

II.

He sat at the table and opened his notes. After a couple of minutes, he got up to drink a glass of water. He switched on the little Phillips transistor he had and tried tuning into some songs.

He then decided it would be more comfortable on the bed. So, took his notes and textbook and pen and sat on the bed. He took one pillow and put it behind his back, the other one he put on his lap.

From under the second pillow fell out a Debonair. He

thought about a suitable place to hide it. He checked out a few articles. He adjusted his lungi. This wasn't working.

He heard a soft tweet in the balcony. He ignored it.

The tweeting grew more persistent. It was night. Birds should be sleeping.

He put the mag under the pillow behind his back and went to investigate.

There were a couple of sparrows carrying grass blades and flying up to grill above his door. They were building a nest there.

One of the sparrows flew awkwardly. Like he had a splint in one of his wings....

III.

He went back to his room. He was feeling drowsy. He did a few stretches. He leaned under his bed. He hid a pack of cigarettes there, so that his wingees couldn't find it. He held the pack in one hand with his thumb and middle finger and with the forefinger of the same hand tapped the bottom of the pack. One cigarette popped out. Perfect!

He lifted the pack and put the projecting cigarette to his lips. In his top drawer he had a pale blue lighter he had bought on a train. He lit the cigarette and kept the lighter flame burning for some time. He put the lighter back in the drawer, tossed the cigarette pack back under the bed and sat on the shorter chair, legs on the bed and blew smoke rings. He surveyed the posters on his wall. Hmmm…

He picked up the day's Indian Express.

He had seen KV guy, Nari and VK do a trick with a lit cigarette and was always envious of them. He decided to practise it.

He flicked the cigarette in the air. It was meant to make an arc in the air and land between his lips. The angle of take-off was too shallow. The ciggy hit the wall behind him.

He tried again with a steeper angle. The force of propulsion was quite high, the ciggy hit the fan blade and deviated on its journey back, landing on the floor next to him.

He tried a third time. This time even as he flicked it, he knew the launch was perfect. It was like when you time a stroke in cricket just right. You know it will make the boundary, long before it actually does!

The ciggy went up, reached its zenith and then started spiralling down. The burning end created a faint continuous glow. Gripping the arms of his chair, he positioned his lips to catch it. Just then the sparrow chirped and distracted him. The ciggy landed on his virgin moustache. He could smell singed hair and tobacco smoke. One hand went to the upper lip to feel the damage. Looked like there was a vacant space in the moustache just below his right nostril.

The smell of singed hair and tobacco grew more pronounced, joined by the smell of burning cloth.

He felt a warmth between his legs.

The ciggy had landed in his lap and burnt a hole in his favourite lungi.

IV.

After the mishap with the lit ciggy, he closed his door and examined the damage. He adjusted his table lamp to get a good view.

He liberally applied Boroline on the affected areas. It was 9:18 pm. The movie would have started.

He gingerly changed into his white pants, put on his purple micro-print satin shirt, combed his hair, adjusted his fringe, dusted his leather chappals, put them on and walked to the Audi. He carried his notes in his hand; maybe during the interval he would study and then do a night out.

He put his movie stub in his pocket. He walked a bit funny as he tried to avoid the burnt areas rubbing against each other. Descending the bhawan stairs was the hardest part.

His chappals made a gentle pit pat on the deserted road. He could hear it louder than usual, because of the eerie calm.

His upper lip itched where his virgin moustache had been singed. He could feel a blister blossoming.

In the dark he walked into something; actually someone…actually two people.

There was a couple walking from the Audi past Ram

Bhawan. They had their arms around each other's shoulders and walked really close.

After the shock of the collision, there was a feminine shriek, followed by a male scream. When they all realised it was an accident, all three said sorry to each other, in three different accents! They went on their way.

V.

He wondered whether the movie was that bad that they were walking away so soon? He wanted to ask, but when he turned around, the couple were walking away arms around each other, staring at the moon above the neem tree canopy. He didn't recognise the girl, he just got a strong smell of jasmine braids, but the guy's camel like gait looked familiar.

A few steps later, he realised that the collision had impacted his singed areas and the pain was brutal. He slowed down his pace. He should have brought the tube of Boroline along. Also, he shouldn't have worn a white pant.

He could now hear the clapping and cheering and banging of chairs in the Audi. There was a song on. His heart started racing.

There was no one at the gate to check his stub. He decided to enter from a side door. He knew where his wingees usually sat.

He entered. It was pitch dark. He put two fingers in his mouth and whistled. There was a delay and then a responding whistle from three rows back.

Gingerly he made his way towards the sound.

He thought he had worked out which row his wingees were. However, they were closer to the aisle and he entered the row from the side.

He couldn't see who was sitting there as he entered the row. He said: "Excuse me" and started his 'journey'. Whoever sat there, wore a lot of clothes!

He got a strong smell of Chanel No 5, followed by Gucci Guilty on the next seat, followed by Black Opium, followed by Jimmy Choo's Blossom, then there was a gap. He took a deep breath and continued. The next one was a scent of Charminar Gulab

Ittar, followed by Daisy, and then Dolce…

There was a torrid scene on the screen and there were a few shouts in multiple languages, accompanied by chair banging asking him to sit down. It was intense, so he retraced his steps and gently lowered himself in the gap between the Charminar Gulab Ittar and Jimmy Choo's Blossom.

His heart was beating fast. Hopefully his Boroline scent would merge into this olfactory feast. His singed areas were feeling scratchy, but he sat still, he dared not touch them. He closed his eyes and just soaked in the atmosphere.

His wingee whistled again wondering where he was. He didn't respond.

VI.

He had been sitting holding his notebook in his lap. He had shrunk his shoulders not wanting to contact his neighbours. A variety of sensations: smell, sound, feelings and emotions were bombarding him.

The variety of scents around him, the rustling of silks, the burning sensation in his singed areas, Sridevi's rain dance caused him to sweat. The knowledge that his friends were a few seats away and free to express themselves didn't help.

He suddenly became conscious of a new but faintly familiar smell coming from the Jimmy Choo lady sitting beside him. Without turning his head, he looked at her surreptitiously from the corner of his eye. In the flashes of light from the screen he saw her sipping from a Coke bottle, a warm glow on her cheeks. He thought he smelt Old Monk but couldn't be sure.

He tried looking at the time on his Timex, wanting to see how far the interval was. It was too dark. He tried bringing his wrist closer to his face. It was too dark. He lowered his hand back gently into his lap being careful not to elbow Jimmy Choo.

Suddenly he was woken from his reverie. He felt something damp and cold on his knee. It was the same Coke bottle. Was she offering it to him, or had she by mistake had parked it on his knee? It was uncomfortable; also, he was worried about his white pants.

He tried gently to nudge the bottle away. The bottle rose in the dark, closer to his chest. Heart pounding, he put his hand around the hand holding the bottle. He felt the bottle being manoeuvred towards his lips.

Just then a message came on screen 'Interval'.

The lights came on.

VII.

The sounds from the screen were replaced by sounds around him.

Chairs were being pushed back as some made their way to the toilets, feet were being stamped on, everyone was talking at the same time. That was the strangest sound. Two thousand people suddenly talking, as if released from their bonds of silence. Some rubbed their eyes from the sudden glare from the ceiling lights, others adjusted their clothes, still others stretched their limbs, backs, necks, other stuff. The aisles were packed. Some moved relaxed, the smokers and toilet goers had a more urgent pace. There were always a few who never came back. They either walked in groups to Nutan, or their rooms, or in the lawns around campus. It was a beautiful night to renew 'friendships'.

Before he got up, he looked around, a bit tentatively. Both CGI and Jimmy Choo ignored him. He got up, notebook in hand and made his way to his long lost wingees. He had a story to tell. He stole a backward glance at the Jimmy Choo girl. Their eyes met briefly, and she looked away, slight smile on her face. Part of him wanted to go back to his seat.

Sigh!

The interval was coming to a close.

He had been out and had a couple of puffs off KV guys' ciggy. KV guy didn't like to share his precious ciggies unless there was a return on investment. KV guy also made a funny face when the ciggy got down to the filter bit.

As he made his way down the aisle, the trailers were on. He made his way to the row his wingees were.

He found his wingees. However, it looked like they had socialised during the break. They had found new friends and the vacant chairs were taken up.

He stood amongst them. The lights were going off and the movie had commenced. People from the rows behind were screaming at him to sit down with newfound energy they had acquired during the break.

Caught in the middle of the row, he struggled on. His singed areas suddenly started feeling increasingly itchy. He passed the CGI girl and mistakenly stamped her toes. He heard a string of choicest Old City Hyderabadi 'words'. How unladylike!

He sat down in his vacant seat next to Jimmy Choo. In the dark, she let out a quiet Rum and Coke burp. How unladylike!

VIII.

As he settled down, he noticed the occupants of the chairs in front had changed.

Occupying the chairs directly in front of him were the EEE couple, Puny and Annie. They were quite distinguishable as Annie had short hair and that aura of a ghotu. Puny was royal and playful at the same time. They were sharing peanuts from the same paper packet. Whilst chivalrous Puny would peel each peanut, he would share the 'peas' with the haughty Annie. Their heads were resting on each other, and partially blocking his view. They were quietly discussing the last Circuit Theory test.

He was feeling lightheaded. Was it KV guy's 'ciggy', he wondered?

CGI next to him was holding her nose. The coke bottle from the Jimmy Choo (JC) girl seemed to have been refilled during the break. Along with feeling lightheaded he was losing his inhibitions.

He tapped JC on the shoulder and asked for a sip. The bottle was half full. He drank the whole lot. CGI was now looking even more disgusted. Even Annie in front was holding her haughty nose.

The mix of new smells: rum and coke, KV guy's ciggy and peanuts was powerfully intoxicating. He leaned on JC's silk clad shoulder and drifted off to sleep.

As he dozed, the movie continued on screen.

Sridevi was now doing PS II at MN Dastur in Calcutta. At the same time Vinod Khanna was doing an extra semester in Pilani.

Vinod was singing a sad song about missing his lady love. He now wore a khadi kurta pyjama with an unshaven face. They kept splashing flashbacks of the couple looking into each other's eyes in Skylab, coochie-cooing at 10:55pm at MB gates, passing notes in Linear Algebra class etc.

He slept through this all...

He woke up with a start. Someone had pinched him.

The Jimmy Choo girl handed him another bottle of 'Coke'. She seemed to have an endless supply.

He felt his singed areas were on fire. He needed Boroline.

Puny and Annie in front were unperturbed. The peanuts were over. Puny was now feeding Annie M&Ms, one at a time.

IX.

The movie was over. The lights came on. The cacophony of moving steel chairs filled the Audi. Drowsy people shared their opinion about the movie with those nearest to them. Some groups hatched plans to go to Nutan.

A guilty conscious gripped him as he clutched his notebook and dreaded the make-up on Monday. He carefully manoeuvred to the aisle and joined the mass exit. He could smell the Coke girl behind him. She was in a hurry and kept pushing him. His way was blocked by a group of three walking abreast ahead of him. All three wore identical denim jackets and were singing Sridevi's rain song in unison.

Stepping out of the main doorway, the cool, fresh air of the night hit him.

Outside the Audi, he turned left, the Coke girl turned right.

X.

He strolled along to his bhawan alone weaving between the throngs that were walking back from the Audi.

The groups walking back were loud in their discussions. It was a cacophony of topics, languages, expressions of boisterousness as they tried to make their voices heard over the others. Occasionally one of the birds resting in the trees above expressed its displeasure by excreting an opinion of its own.

He passed by a group discussing the Jimmy Choo girl who had sat next to him. He slowed down behind them to keep pace. Whilst one was proudly mentioning how she had sat beside him in class, another spoke about sitting across her in the Library, yet another had run after her a week ago to give her the pen she had dropped whilst parking her cycle. Still another said that there were rumours she had been spotted late night at C'Not with a senior from Krishna Bhawan.

There was a 'pregnant' lull in their discussion; a few silent sighs…. until someone brought up Sridevi's rain dance.

He quickened his pace and overtook them, tightly clutching his notebook at his side.

From experience he walked in the middle of the road. Though it annoyed the cyclists, the probability of bird droppings was relatively lesser.

XI.

Meanwhile, he had reached his Bhawan. His singed areas were singing for attention and Boroline.

As he passed KV guy's room he paused. KV guy was in his room which was a rarity. Most nights KV guy crashed wherever he found himself after midnight.

KV guy had a new framed poster on the wall. It was a portrait of an IBM 3000, with a couple of incense sticks burning at its base.

KV guy was busy. His mattress had been laid out on the floor and a mosaic of punch cards was placed on the wooden bed. The bed itself had been moved to the middle of the room, so as to give KV guy access all along the perimeter.

The normally subdued KV guy was charged up as he darted this way and that, rearranging his punch cards. Occasionally, he scratched his mop (which was eyeing the Clinic Plus on the window with dread); said WTF in a T Nagar accent. He then found a reclusive card, kissed it for luck and placed it strategically on the bed. Behind his ears were two Wills Navy Cut cigarettes, one with a squeezed end; preventing the contents from falling out.

Up to KV guy's room sauntered the Marathas: Chowder and Niger.

Chowder looked around the room for food, found none, thought it was too hot and switched on the fan!

Some people say it was the loudest WTF they ever heard in a T Nagar accent as the punch cards flew around the room.

XII.

The next morning, he woke early. Rather he was woken. There was a commotion outside his room. He gingerly got up to investigate.

He could see the dhobi's bundle on the balcony. The sounds were coming from nearer the stairs where there was a group huddled discussing something animatedly.

Vivek was squatting on his haunches besides the dhobi and the chowki. They were both staring at something and arguing. As the first rays of the sun fell on the object, it looked to be Cookie's 'third' tennis ball.

There was a stain on the ball, which Vivek couldn't remove. The normally calm, peaceable Vivek was anxious and worried, possibly with lack of sleep. The dhobi wanted to take the ball to the 'ghat' with him and beat it with a 'bat'; however, Vivek did not want to part with it. Besides him lay a soap dish with an unsuccessfully used 'Rin'.

Standing beside Vivek and the dhobi was Chumma in his Rupa banyan and pyjamas. In one hand he held a lota, with the other he held a 'Classic' ciggie. The ciggie hand gesticulated as he offered advice. Occasionally, the ciggie hand would also gently massage his tummy as he 'built up pressure'. Chumma asked Vivek why he was so bothered with the stain. He said: "Fundamentally, the dynamics and properties of the ball would remain unaffected by the stain. You wouldn't notice any difference while playing. Also, the ball wasn't designed for aesthetic appeal." As usual, Chumma's advice wasn't taken.

Singh from Muzaffarpur sauntered down and squatted next to the group. He offered his 'gamcha' to clean the ball; however, he was ignored as well. He offered to 'acquire' a new ball for Vivek from the Tennis Club Captain who owed Singh a non-mentionable favour.

D M from Kurnool came over. DM was an early riser. He had showered, been to the temple, had breakfast in the mess and was returning with his bottle of 'gunpowder pudi'.

DM was also working on learning Hindi, one of the reasons he had opted for a room in this wing. He walked up to the group and began framing his question in his mind. He asked: "Vivek, tera ball dirty hai?" (Vivek: is your ball dirty?)

He strolled back to his room. He was still dazed. The night's events, the notebooks reminding him of the test the next day, the blisters and being woken up rather abruptly, the stained ball… Too much!

XIII.

His white pants from the night before were slumped on his chair. As he moved to put them away, he found something pink projecting from one of the pockets. He gently pulled it out. It was a neatly folded ladies' handkerchief with a red border, printed with teddy bears holding balloons and a blue 'S' crocheted. It had a distinct Jimmy Choo smell. He wondered when she had slipped it into his pockets. Must have been when he was dozing.

Now he was excited. The pain from the singed areas was forgotten, the test not important anymore; could he tell his friends?

Why did she do it? Did she want him to return it to her at MB? A thousand thoughts…

Heart beating fast, he decided to hide the kerchief before any of his wingees walked in. He put it under his mattress in between the pages of the latest Debonair.

It didn't feel right keeping it there. So, he took it out and put it back in his white pant pockets. No one would look there.

He quickly had a bath. The singe areas burnt; he didn't care. He walked to the mess for breakfast. Usually on Sundays, the whole wing went together; today was different. He hurriedly ate and went back to his room to look at the kerchief again. He had never been to MB before. He didn't know her name; how could he return it? He felt deflated.

Feeling a little guilt, as if he was invading her privacy, he opened the folded kerchief. Scribbled in the centre was: Skylab 10:00 am.

He looked at his watch. It was 9.50 am.

He changed quickly and ran down the stairs and out of the Bhawan. He realised that he had left the kerchief in his room. He ran up again.

At the turn of the stairs he crashed into SAK wearing a rainbow T-shirt and lycra shorts. SAK was contesting for the Hostel Cultural-Secretary elections and was handing out fliers (on punch cards) with his manifesto.

The crash spilled the punch cards on the stairs. SAK wasn't happy. He thought this was a deliberate act from his rival contestant to derail his campaign. He let out a string of accented expletives learnt in a boarding school at the foothills of the Himalayas.

Having retrieved the kerchief, he ran down the stairs again having to avoid the still ruffled SAK who was trying to collect his punch cards bent over at an awkward angle.

At the bottom of the stairs, he found SAK's bicycle parked. He decided to 'borrow' it.

The bike was clean, well-oiled and beautifully maintained. He reached Sky in exactly two minutes.

He leaned the bike on the bushes and looked around....in dismay. It was quite a different Skylab than he expected.

A school group was visiting the Museum and 200 or so kids were running around the lawns, shrieking, rolling in the grass, hurling twigs at each other, eating. It was chaos. A couple of kids had already found SAK's bike and were giving it close, robust attention. The bike didn't look clean, well-oiled and well maintained anymore.

A couple of teachers came up to him with a camera and asked him to click a photo of the staff. They took five minutes to organise themselves. He was losing time.

He handed the camera back, craning his neck to find her. He couldn't spot any BITSian. He thought about asking Pappu.

Then it happened!

He became aware of the now familiar scent around him, as he breathed hard and fast.

Time seemed to stop. The noises of the kids and the general chaos seemed to disappear.

He felt her presence…

He felt the kerchief gently being pulled out of his pocket. As if in a trance, he turned around and…

… and looked into the most beautiful, smiling, deep pair of eyes he had ever imagined….

XIV.

He looked into her eyes, mesmerised, not knowing what to say, or do.

Somehow his mind switched back to his fresher days and he blurted: My name is …., from Trichy…! My ID is 83A3PS…

She just continued smiling cool, composed, confident; whilst he fidgeted. He put his hands in his pockets, removed them out, put them behind his back, put them in his pocket again.

He finally built up his courage and asked: "Shikhanji?"

She replied: "Cheeku shake?"

They walked to Pappu's counter; he maintaining an awkward space between them.

He ordered a shikhanji and a cheeku shake, then discovered he hadn't brought any money.

Pappu had seen and been through countless such encounters and guessed his discomfiture. He just smiled at him and said: "Baad mein?" (Later?)

He nodded. Pappu said he would send the drinks over with his chottu.

He led her towards a quiet spot. Trying to keep a respectable distance and looking at her surreptitiously from the corner of his eye, he nearly tripped into a pool of water.

She reached out her hand, grabbed his elbow and steadied him. He was embarrassed.

Keeping a hand on his elbow, she guided him to a shady spot and sat down. He sat down awkwardly, again his singed areas making squatting difficult.

In a daze, he looked around, looked at her, looked at Pappu's counter, looked at her, looked at the museum, looked at her.

As they sat sipping their drinks, the conversation was erratic at best. Whilst she nursed her cheeku shake, he had finished his shikhanji and was sipping the 'water' from the melting ice, trying to dodge a couple of lime seeds which had escaped Pappu's sieve.

Pappu's chottu came on his rounds and relieved him off his glass. Now he had nothing to distract him.

Her cheeku shake looked interesting. Once when she was sipping, her eyes looking at the glass, he looked at her full lips and his imagination went wild.

He coloured up. She asked whether he was ok. He said, Yes.

He wasn't good at this. He needed to get some coaching from a guy who was in the p wing in his bhawan and occasionally drifted down to their wing.

Maltese was 'suave' personified. Elegant in all that he did and wore, even down to his gold rimmed glasses and fashionably receding hairline embellished with a MChats accent.

Maltese usually came to borrow a newspaper or when he caught the whiff of Maggi being cooked in any room. Maltese always brought his own spoon.

During these visits Maltese would wax eloquent about his 'exploits' and 'success' in relationships with the fairer sex. According to Maltese himself, he was well known and revered with a seasoned track record in the corridors of Delhi's JMC, LSR, LHMC, IP and MH.

Maltese had a universal theory on how to initiate contact, nurture a relationship through the early stages of germination, have the right engagement thereafter to have a balanced relationship so as to meet his goals, and then when all had been achieved to have a smooth exit strategy.

He had disinterestedly heard Maltese's discourses, thinking he would never need them, and even bluntly denied Maltese a spoon of his Maggi on many an occasion.

However, now that he needed it, he would cook some Maggi tonight and have a session with 'Maltese'.

The cheeku shake meanwhile was about half finished. It was nearing lunch time.

He had visions of purees, pulao, mutter-paneer and cassata ice-cream. It made him smile. He looked at his watch.

She asked him: "Ki holo?" (What happened?)

He arched his eyebrows questioningly.

She asked: "Why are you smiling?"

He felt embarrassed. He said: "Kuch nahi. Aisseech!" (Nothing. Just like that).

She arched her eyebrows questioningly.

He changed the topic.

"What time does the mess open in MB?" he asked.

Through his next few questions, he found out they had a similar menu and similar timings, however her enthusiasm for the purees, pulao, mutter-paneer and cassata was far less than his.

His mind went back to three weeks ago. His sidee had gone late for Sunday 'grub' and had trouble finding any paneer in the last bowl of mutter paneer, the purees were more like papads and the cassata was over.

He couldn't let that happen. However, he didn't want to end this time either. His mind hurt with indecision. His singed areas felt scratchy.

But then, the 'outside the box thinking' culture of the place, nurtured over the generations kicked in.

He told her he had a make-up test the next day. She apparently had one too. Same course as well.

XV.

They got up, dusted themselves and walked out of Sky.

Pappu gave him a thumbs up on the way out. Pappu's chottu winked at him.

The school kids were getting into their bus; their teachers frantically counting them. Pandemonium!

Whilst his heart wanted to be with her, his tummy was rumbling with visions of the Sunday grub. The tummy won. He said bye. He forgot about the 'borrowed' cycle and walked back. He cast a look behind. She was getting on her cycle.

As she disappeared from his view, he increased his pace

and then broke off into a jog. As he jogged, he extended his arms, like an airplane and zig zagged through the street under the lazy canopy of the noon neem trees. His steps were light, his feet in the clouds.

As he passed the warden's house, he saw the would-be Cultural-Secretary coming out. He then remembered about the 'borrowed' bike. However, more urgent matters beckoned.

He waltzed into the mess; got onto the next available table, next to guys he hardly knew; secured his properly blown up hot purees, and more than adequate ratio of paneer to mutter, enjoyed the steaming hot pulao with raisins, washed down with cool water from a jug, signalled a mess servant for the cassata ice cream, swallowed it; burped with gastronomic pleasure, collected a fistful of saunf and waltzed out of the mess.

Both of them didn't do too well at the make-up test and somehow didn't pursue things further.

Wingees

They say it takes a village to bring up a child; well, wingees have an effect too.

Being a second semmer, doing a C group course alone, PS1 friendships, gym, etc., created a random experience for Ajmeri with at least 4 sets of wingees with rather distinct characteristics during his time in BITS. Each set left a mark on him and added to the rich experience of life in Pilani.

First term, he was in the Shankar lower back wing with Biharis for sidees and a Bihari backie. Life was interesting to say the least, as he was exposed to the Bihari culture for the first time. Ragging stopped after the first two weeks as seniors stopped picking freshers from their wing as these guys had built a 'reputation'.

The next year he was again with seven Biharis in the upstairs wing facing the Shankar-Vyas mess, along with close second semester three non-Bihari friends. These three were his sane company in the otherwise fast-moving world of the Bihari wingees: talk about politics, wardens and plenty of after dark activities. One of them being elected mess-secretary added to the heady mix. It ended when the Biharis' rooms in his wing were burnt.

Moving on, since the Biharis were expelled; his other wingees moved into wings with their course mates; one of them left Pilani. Ajmeri was allocated a room by default (happens to friendless people) with the 83 first semester C group guys in VK Bhawan. Life was ok, but he didn't really gel with these guys. No fault of theirs but almost all of them were from the south, and he couldn't impose on them to speak in English all the time when they were more at ease in their native language.

The summer vacation before that Ajmeri had met SRK and Chumma at PS 1 and formed strongish friendships. So, in the second semester of that year, he joined them in Bhagirath. Great bunch of guys. Hindi and when drunk, Punjabi was the language of the wing. Compared with the sedate C group guys in VK, this was a loud wing, amplified with Dukki procuring a 100-watt music system from Bubba.

The year after was again a change of scenery. Half the Bhagirath mob were going on PS2 and the other half wanted to do well with their CGPA and cut down on the 'fun' element. Ajmeri landed among a bunch of high achieving second semester EEE guys in Ashok. The average CGPA of the wing at that time was 8.9. Ajmeri getting elected RPA mess-secretary and Security Co-ordinator for Oasis and BITS games reduced this slightly, to about 8.5. These were heady days. Prof. SSR was revered as he was the EEE guru and also the warden of Ashok Bhawan.

The Rehri (Street Food Cart)

Lala pushed the rehri into the campus. The rehri was fully loaded for the evening business. A couple of bells at the edges tinkled in the hot afternoon sun. As it passed by Ashok and Bhagirath, it was subliminally heard subconsciously in a few ears; ears belonging to some, who lived in constant dislike of the mess food. For them, without Nagar's rehri, Blue Moon, Skylab and Bank Canteen, life would be unbearable on the campus (gastronomically at least).

Lala was not used to pushing carts. He struggled with the misbalanced load, the misaligned wheels, the lack of lubricant in the hub, the melting tar of the hot afternoon roads, the red Coke metal icebox precariously balanced on the right corner of the cart, and his owns chappal straps pulling on his feet.

Nagar and his chottu followed behind the cart holding the trays of samosas and the bag of limes respectively. They were in no hurry. They had started early knowing they had an amateur pushing the cart. Chottu chortled in glee, for some reason he found the scene of a third-year engineering student pushing the rehri funny; he also found the unsynchronised undulations of Lala's gait funny.

Lala didn't think it funny at all.

They reached the spot of business. Lala placed some stones at the base of the wheels to keep the cart stable. From the shelf under the cart he removed the stack of moodas and spread them out. Next, he swept out the sidewalk where customers would sit. He then took two buckets and walked to Bhagirath new wing bogs to collect water. One bucket was used for shikhanji; the other was used to wash the glasses.

Customers started drifting in and Nagarji commenced business in earnest.

Lala took out his little notebook and got Nagarji to sign it.

Lala had two more weeks of this work to pay off his debt for the previous semester.

...

Meanwhile, Gundu was passing by on his evening pre dinner solitary constitutional.

His walking route changed day to day, but there were some fixed landmarks he made sure were not bypassed; e.g. MB gates, temple lawns, Skylab perimeter, mess quarters in RPA, Swimming Pool and Nagar's rehri.

On this particular day, he stopped by the rehri; folded up his silk dhoti, patted down his luxurious moustache and enquired of Nagar's chottu about the 'gos' on his sidee Lala.

Chottu didn't say anything. He just made a sign like squeezing limes for shikhanji...

Notes

Early morning Leonie rode out on her bike from MB to 'borrow' notes from Nguyen.

She would usually stand outside front wing Bhagirath and ask anyone wandering in the wings to knock on Nguyen's door. Today, the wing wore a deserted look.

As she waited, she noticed a few steel glasses lying in the corridor. There were a couple of upturned plastic buckets, and a small smouldering pile of ashes where two chairs had met a 'bon-firey' end in the lawn between the corridor and the hedge.

Then she remembered.

Nguyen had mentioned Wonky had given a birthday treat the previous night.

She needed those notes. She had a make up the next day!

Leonie picked up some small stones and threw them at Nguyen's door. Her aim wasn't good. She heard a string of abuses in Telegu, Tamil and Punjabi, before a stone hit the correct door and Polynesian swear words escaped.

A mess servant, Giri, wandered past collecting the steel tumblers from the corridor and almost got caught in the stone spray.

On her directions, Giri knocked on 120 persistently, patiently weathering the swearing and threats, until Nguyen opened the door wearing only a towel.

Bleary eyed, he tried to push Giri away. He hadn't noticed Leonie on the road.

Giri tried to tell him about her. Nguyen didn't comprehend. In the scuffle, the towel loosened and fell off.

There was a shriek from the road.

Only then did Nguyen realise he had a visitor.

Ladka aur ladki (Boy and Girl)

Oasis 1988

83 batch ladka bunked a few days from PSII and came to Pilani for Oasis.

The day Ladka reached Pilani he went to C'Not looking for familiar ladka faces. He ran into a junior ladki who was in the same branch as he. The ladki said hello and had a few questions about PS II, job prospects, etc. Ladki invited ladka for a cheeku shake.

Ladka had never sat with any ladki alone in C'Not or anywhere. This was new ground.

Long story short, after an hour or two ladka and ladki decided to meet next morning to attend some key Oasis events.

The day was long. Ladka was discovering what he had missed all these years. Ladka's other ladka friends winked at him whenever he walked past them.

Evening came, and ladka and ladki had dinner in C'Not.

Three and a half years of gossip hype then took over. Ladka tried to steer ladki into some deserted lawns between events. Ladki was too smart. Finally, ladka dropped ladki at MB at some late hour. (MB curfew hours were relaxed during Oasis).

Next morning ladka woke up and realised that this was not what Oasis was about. He found his ladka friends and spent the next four days, drinking and generally getting 'wasted'.

Great last Oasis for the ladka!!!

Morning after the pageant

Ratan Lal was on his mid-morning cycling constitutional.

Passing the Institute, he noticed Aggro and his friends sitting on a dharna outside the Audi. He stopped his cycle and walked up to a parked rickshaw wallah who was smoking a beedi. Borrowing a light, Ratan Lal squatted besides the rickshaw wallah and enquired what the protest was about.

He was advised that there had been a scandal. At the gala the previous night, the wrong girl had been crowned Miss MB!

Jay who was the MC had made an 'error' apparently and had crowned Miss Delhi as Miss MB, instead of the favourite Miss Trivandrum.

Miss Trivandrum had clearly won the swimsuit round held

at the swimming pool and the traditional costume round. Miss Delhi, despite being the 'hot' favourite had faltered on the maths quiz, confused about the odds and evens.

Ratan Lal finished his smoke, nodded to the rickshaw wallah, adjusted his dhoti and sanpha, got on his bike, rubbed his belly once, rang the bell on his bike and continued with his morning constitutional...

He had lost interest in the gala, ever since 'N' had been knocked out in the earlier rounds.

Meeting at Mandir

He was late. Panic set in. He was to meet her at the Mandir lawns at 2.00pm!

He ran to his room to change. The morning session in Sky had left some grass stains on his pants. As he ran up the stairs, Mal ran with him, wondering what the hurry was about.

He blurted a quick summary. Mal got it straight away, having travelled the delicate, yet pulsating, pathways of new love before.

He changed into new pants and a 'Proline' T shirt, which had freshly arrived from the dhobi that morning. The crease was still sharp. He checked himself in the mirror, grabbed his notebook and ran down the stairs. Mal had flagged down and commandeered a passing rickshaw for him. He jumped on, flashed a thumbs up to Mal and was off, goading the rickshaw wallah to speed up.

He dared not look at his watch, yet he flashed a backwards glance at the clock tower. It was 2.45 pm. He was very late!

He jumped off the rickshaw, shouted a 'baad mien' (pay you later) and ran into the Mandir lawns.

Breathless, he stopped!

He didn't know where to start looking for her. He thought about calling out, but besides not knowing her name, he didn't want to embarrass either her or himself.

He walked around the perimeter of the lawns. There were a few couples relaxing in the lawns. Imli and Jay had a Jaipuri razai (quilt) spread out as a picnic mat. Whilst Imli lay down with her white chunni shielding her face, Jay was keeping flies away with a little Japanese punkah which had images of geishas.

Chumma and KV guy, were lying down parallelly head to toe (Chumma's head near KV guy's toes and vice versa) next to each other discussing whether pyjamas or lungis were more comfortable as nightwear.

Some GKWs were collected in a corner, smoking beedis contentedly. They had mowed the lawns, leaving a 3'x7' patch where Gor and Khushi were practicing Allahabadi Pilates.

II.

He couldn't find her.

Surely, she had come and gone. He was dejected.

Behind the temple he found a quiet, lonely spot, sat down, opened his notebook, looked at the sky and decided to study.

He became aware of the fragrance of the freshly cut grass. The jasmine blooms near the temple wafted their fresh scent towards him riding the gentle afternoon breeze. There was a remnant of incense smoke from the morning puja at the temple which hung as a haze in the surrounds.

This gentle cocktail of scents lifted his spirits slightly. He closed his eyes.

There was a new yet familiar scent that joined this mix. He looked around but couldn't see her. Was his mind playing tricks on him?

He saw and heard a slight rustle in the bushes to his right.

Something soft and squishy hit him on his forehead and fell into his lap. It was a ripe nimboli. (neem tree fruit).

He knew she was there.

III.

Meanwhile, Vivek had a Sunday routine.

He got up before dawn, swept his room, dusted the posters on his wall, trimmed his facial hair, had an early breakfast, came back to his room and arranged his tennis gear.

He paid close attention to the tennis balls, arranging them in order of use. The cricket fanatics were always approaching him for used balls. They had learnt his system of arrangement and could tell at a glance whether he had any to spare.

Vivek changed his bedspreads and arranged his pens, drafter, FX-82, textbooks, notebooks, birthday cards, 'magazines' and lastly ticked off the date on his countdown sheet - counting the days to the end of the sem.

By this time his wingees were waking up and taking leisurely strolls to the bogs, reading the Sunday newspaper in the sun. It was picture of relaxation in the wing.

Vivek then heated two buckets of water. Sunday baths were extra-long and luxurious. He sang as he lifted the two buckets to the bogs. So graceful was his gait, not a drop spilled on the way.

In a little while his wingees heard Rafi and Kishore songs emanating from the bogs. Yodelling was also heard as the water got cold.

After an early lunch, Vivek would lie down on his bed, and read the sports section of the Indian Express cover to cover, especially ruminating on articles on umpiring. He would drop off to a gentle nap.

Around 2.30pm, Vivek would wake up and don his running gear. He wore his tennis headband, adjusted it so that the Nike symbol was right in front on the forehead and did some stretches and set out on his hour-long jog. By habit, he ran the perimeter of the mandir lawns to start with.

Today, as he ran, he jumped over the 'parallel pair' Chumma and the KV guy, jogged past Jay and Imli; Jay waved his geisha fan, and stumbled into a guy nursing a 'nimboli' bruise on his forehead.

The impact landed him into the bushes nearby, into something soft, silky and fragrant…and soft.

After a lull, a scream was heard.

IV.

Vivek watched the commotion in the bushes but found himself frozen by the sudden events.

Jay on the other hand had heard the scream, and with generations of chivalrous DNA in his bloodstream, reacted quickly. He was off his feet in a quick, lithe move and racing towards the source of the scream.

Jay's view was hidden partially by the bush. He could see Vivek extricate himself from the tangle without his glasses, which had been knocked off and were lying near Jay's feet.

Vivek, without his glasses, reached out to lift the lady up. He reached out for her arm and got a stinging slap on his wrist. What he had thought was her hand turned out not to be her hand.

As Vivek grimaced with pain and embarrassment, Jay handed him his glasses. Vivek put them on and adjusted his Nike headband.

She was slowly rising, and both Vivek and Jay turned around so that she could settle herself and her clothes with dignity.

Meanwhile Imli who had dozed off, felt the heat of the sun on her face and wondered why the 'fanning' had stopped.

Finding Jay missing, she was puzzled. This was highly unlike him. She stood up, dusted herself, said "Hmph" and walked around the temple.

From a distance she could see Jay on his knees fanning a girl with dishevelled hair and clothes.

V.

Vivek stood there watching the scene.

There wasn't much movement, but the undercurrents were strong. The breeze had gone still, the birds held their fire (excretions), even the bees stopped buzzing. It looked like nature had paused.

Jay could feel the tension. He folded the geisha fan. With the other hand, he pulled down his shirt behind him to cover his exposed tattoo.

He could hear a crunch as Imli bit into an apple. He knew she was somewhere behind him, maybe leaning against a tree as was her wont, one arm on her waist, eyes icy cold.

He turned around slowly, trying to get his story right. It was as he had imagined. The sun was behind her back casting a long grey shadow on the grass.

His palms became sweaty. He shivered momentarily. The sun was filtering through her white kurta, highlighting her tensed muscles.

She bit the apple again. The crunch was loaded with restrained anger.

The girl rose from the bush and walked towards her study companion. They both stood watching Imli and Jay.

Imli turned away with another 'Hmph' and walked away, tossing the half-eaten apple over her shoulder. Jay followed.

Vivek stretched his hamstrings, wiped his glasses, put them on and with a wave to no one in particular, jogged away.

The bees buzzed once again.

The mess- 'servant'

Every morning at about 6:45am the grizzled old man would take his place behind the counter on the non-veg side of the mess. Next to him was a stack of egg trays. The eggs weren't that clean; some feathers and hen poo stuck to some of them. In front of him was a gas stove and a gas cylinder next to it. To the other side was a stack of steel plates.

The old man fried eggs for breakfast.

The mess closed for breakfast at 9:00 am. So from 7 to 9 am he sat there in his dark blue faded 'mess servant' uniform and fried hundreds of eggs continuously.

Summers he sweated; winters the warmth of the stove was welcome.

The 'serving' mess servants would take orders from the tables and relay it to the old man. The staple orders were half-fry, full fry, French toast and omelette. The French toast was just slices of bread fried in a beaten-up egg; the omelette was a fried beaten-up egg. Occasionally, someone would order an extra: a cheese omelette. What that meant was, he would chop a cube of Amul cheese and add to a beaten-up egg and fry it as an omelette. The other rare variety was when Ajmeri would walk up from a morning gym session and have him break up six eggs into a steel glass and gobble it up. Only then he'd look up from his stove and give a glimmer of a smile.

The inmates were students. They came from various backgrounds.

Cracking hundreds of eggs, his nails were dark and greasy. No one minded the dirt and the grease too much. Not many noticed the old man too much. They were upset if their eggs were delayed or not properly done. They vented at the 'server' mess servants or the mess manager. They didn't speak to the old man. He just sat there and fried eggs.

During lunch and dinner the old man had different duties in the kitchen. The students didn't know what they were. They didn't really care.

In between meals, the old man retired to the 'mess servants' quarters behind the mess. Mornings, he was back at work. Seven days a week.

His family was in a village far away. He visited them when the Institute was closed for summer.

He did this year after year. Winter, summer, rain, sunshine. Servant quarters, mess kitchen, egg frying pan was his world.

The students would be there 4-5 years and scatter around the world. Most would earn their millions, most would stay in touch with friends they sat at the mess tables: WhatsApp groups, reunions, kid's weddings.

The old man...well, he was just a mess servant.

Random sound bites from 83-87

Giri, Chapati chahaiye
Manager ko bulao
Postie has come machaan
Oye Backie, shut up...I'm trying to sleep
What's in the mess today yaar?
Can I borrow a fag?
Bhaiyya, bus stand jaa rahe hain hum

Ki khobor, dada?
You got a pen ra?
Saaley dhobi ne fir pyjamey ka naada ghuma diya
Nice movie in Blue Moon
Pappu ek shikhanji aur ek chotta gold flake
Yeh kya Tamil/Telegu mein batiyaate rehte hain…
Oye Chup, DeshP aa raha hai
Kal Compree hai; **** phat rahi hai
Silk Smitha Movie in Audi Ra
Fresher ja raha hai
Pass me the tumbler

Love was…

Sharing someone's bowl of Maggi

Having a sip from someone's milk shake

Having a puff of the communal ciggie/ chillum/ reefer

The smell of chlorine infused damsels cycling past

The 'Archies' poster of Madhubala staring at you from the wall

Sharing a workshop assignment with the glamorous and the beautiful

Having the last sip from the Old Monk bottle (before dropping a lit match into it for that 'whoosh' sound).

Jat helping you with the last rep on the bench press

Sharing your saunf on your way back from the mess

The long silent march to the campus after a 'late-night' movie at Nihali chowk

Hearing the dulcet tones of Penaaz Masani

The 'almost' dulcet tones of a wingee singing in the shower

The 10.30 pm march to MB from C'Not with your lady friend, trying (unsuccessfully) for a pit stop at Shiv Ganga and/ or Mandir lawns

Having the freedom to walk around in the wing wrapped in a towel

25 years later, being called a juvenile brat.

The batch farewells Pilani

They sat in a corner of C'Not by themselves. It was early evening on May 14th, 1987. The hot sun, they didn't mind.

Passers-by stared; they didn't care anymore.

They didn't speak much, they just stared past each other's shoulders. Occasionally, their eyes met, lingered and moved away.

In the past those lingering eye contacts had held promise, challenge, exploration and at times youthful passions.

Today, it was more of betrayal; this was the last time they were together. The next morning, her dad's car would whisk her away; he would catch a bus to Delhi.

Partings are never easy. Memories flashed past. Sitting beside each other in the Audi, long walks to and from MB, meeting in Sky, occasional tiffs and not talking for a few days; patching up, the pain of missing each other during the holidays, the joy of reuniting on the first day of each term. Memories.

Neither wanted this time to end.

On the other hand, sitting together, knowing it was the last time, made it harder.

As usual, she took the decision. This time she wanted to walk back to Meera Bhawan alone. She said bye, no handshake, no hug, nothing. She just picked up her bag and walked away.

At the corner of Shiv Ganga, she glanced back at C'Not. He stood there under a tree watching her. He looked frail and lonesome.

She turned away and continued walking.

II.

December, 1988

It was evening. It was cold at Nutan Bus stand.

The five second-semmers sat on their moodas huddled around a large bowl of smouldering charcoal. The bowl was a round iron tray, the kind used by labourers to carry sand, cement, bricks, etc.

They were all in kurta pyjamas. They covered themselves with thick shawls. The pyjamas were once white, but four years of dhobi washings had made them more cream than white.

All smoked, lighting one cigarette at a time and passing it around the circle. One of them was constantly licking his lips, so the person next to him usually got a 'wet' cigarette. They didn't mind.

The passing buses and tempos blew swirls of dust around them. They didn't mind.

Occasionally embers from the coal would rise and land on their shawls. They dusted them off. They didn't mind.

A stray dog came and lay next to one of the moodas. They didn't mind.

They had had two chais each already. The glasses from the last round still lay at their feet. The traffic around the bus stop had thinned as the last bus had left for the night. The locals including the rickshaw wallahs were going home for the night.

The five sat in silence. They looked at the smouldering coal intently.

They smoked.

Their hearts felt heavy, throats dry.

Tomorrow they would all leave the campus, maybe forever.

Maybe their paths would cross later in life. Maybe they'd never see each other again.

Either way.

It would never be the same again.

III.

The three of them stood at Nutan waiting for the bus.

Mal was going to Delhi to spend a couple of weeks with his folks, before heading off to the US for his MBA.

KV Guy was staying back another couple of days; he hadn't got a train reservation from Delhi to Trichy until two days later. He would return to Pilani next semester anyway. He was doing a dual degree.

Ratan Lal had a bus in three hours to Jaipur. He had brought his luggage to Nutan. He had got a job in Bombay with Hindustan Levers. The job commenced in 4 weeks. His folks in Jaipur were arranging for him to 'see' some girls in those 4 weeks.

They had come to Nutan a couple of hours early. Mal and Ratan Lal had shared a rickshaw, piling all their luggage. The rickshaw guy had walked the rickshaw whilst the three of them had held the luggage in place. Hiring one rickshaw had saved them ten rupees.

They had bought beers at the 'wine' shop and drank them slowly. They shared a bottle at a time. So too with the cigarettes. One was lit and passed around at a time. The cigarette was smoked until the fire touched the filter.

They wished time would slow down. They had been wingees and friends for three years now. They had gone to the mess together, studied night outs together, watched movies in Audi, Dabba, and behind Blue Moon together. They had missed each other over the long summer breaks and rejoiced seeing each other when semesters began.

It was coming to an end.

They had exchanged addresses; knowing they most probably wouldn't really write.

They avoided eye contact. The Delhi bus arrived. They loaded Mal's luggage on the bus. They shook hands, looked so formal. Mal got his seat, waved from the window as the bus rolled out of the bus stand, and then slowly disappeared down the road, leaving behind just dust.

And…

…a slight pain in the heart, slight reddening in the eyes…no tears…that wouldn't be 'manly'…all three separated...

It would never be the same again.

IV.

And the last one from the batch says farewell…

After the last compree, he walked down the wing to his room.

All the rooms were empty. His wingees had finished their comprees a day or two earlier and had left. He was leaving the next morning.

The empty rooms looked eerie.

Gone were the bedding, the music systems, the books, the curtains, the clothes, cigarettes and the posters...especially the posters.

Gone were his friends...it was so quiet.

He had to walk alone to the mess for dinner, eat alone, and walk back to his own room alone.

His cases were packed. No ties left to this place.

The ties would just be memories now.

Memories he would cherish.

Forever...

Part 2.
After Pilani

Singapore

Every Saturday morning, he has his breakfast on the balcony.

Wearing a faded white kurta pyjama and hawai chappals. Lydia, his Filipino maid, brings him a small steel plate with a cube of frozen butter and a blob of jam.

She also hands him a couple of slices of half burnt toast and a jug of tea with a steel glass.

Using his iPhone compass, he turns to face the direction of the BITS clock tower and eats his breakfast.

II.

She sat on her hotel balcony sipping her room service delivered Sing-Sing cocktail.

It has been a long day; the tropical humidity had sapped energy and left her dehydrated.

The evening sea breeze was refreshing. She had kicked off her shoes and rested her feet on the balcony railings. On the balcony next door, a transvestite was practicing a pole dancing routine. It looked a bit odd without the make-up and costume.

She just muttered an "Hmph" under her breath and continued sipping her cocktail.

Her phone buzzed with a WhatsApp message. She ignored it.

The marina was a hive of activity. A cruise ship flying an SG flag had docked a bit away from the shore and boats were ferrying passengers to the shore, where touts offered visits to 'delightful' and exotic venues.

Her eyes were drawn to an Austin Powers lookalike, who got off a limousine that had just pulled up. The chauffer was in red livery.

Something looked familiar about Austin's gait. She watched him walk in his chinos and sunhat, a designer leather bag across his chest, a couple of 'exec' suits respectfully leading the way.

They walked to a section of the Marina where a number of yachts were parked. They led 'Austin' to a particularly slick looking, large yacht. He disappeared below deck with them.

Intrigued, she slipped out a pair of binoculars from her purse and zoomed in.

Next to the yacht was a full-sized poster of Daniel Craig in a Bond pose. The boat may have been used in a Bond movie.

The scene, the evening breeze and the cocktail, had worked up a light sweat all over her body; she wiped it off with a scarf.

Austin appeared on the deck of the boat and she recognised him. She was surprised it took her so long.

It came back to her. The trips to their hometown in the Amby, the occasional meet up at C'Not and Sky, MB nights and more recently, his appearance on business TV channels.

She watched as he was led to the sun deck by a couple of local models in the latest Parisian beachwear.

III.

SR had recently moved to SG. He was getting used to the sights and sounds. SG already had well established star 83 batch presence: A TV star (ATVS).

LMA had dropped in from India for a visit to SG, and as was customary as well as a 33-year tradition organised to spend some time with the ATVS.

Being a gracious personality and with some prompting/ blackmailing/ persuasion from a certain imp Down Under, ATVS had invited SR to the dinner with LMA.

SR had arrived a bit late opting to wear a black non-committal Lacoste T-shirt that contrasted his greying locks and set off his rosy tropical infused cheeks effectively.

He found ATVS and LMA deep in conversation. ATVS looked like a typical corporate honcho after a long day: crumpled designer shirt with gold monogrammed cufflinks, tie fashionably askew.

SR stood in the shadows at a distance and took in the

surroundings. ATVS wasn't his normal confident self; he sat on the edge of the chair, nervously looking at the napkin, drawing lines on the condensation on his beer glass.

The froth had flattened in the beer; it didn't look sipped. LMA was twirling a lock on the side of her head with a finger, talking with a low voice, looking at the menu card.

She lifted her eyes and saw SR. She nodded. SR shuffled over, with a breezy: "Kya haal hai mitron?" (How are you friends?)

He pulled his chair and settled down, surreptitiously loosening his belt under the table. He did that before every meal.

ATVS looked relieved and signalled Julie, the waitress to get SR a beer.

The beer came over. LMA, always organised and protocol minded, asked Julie to take a picture of the three of them. As they turned to face Julie, SR noticed ATVS' strained smile…

… he also noticed; ATVS' right ear was red!

IV.

Cynthia Tan sat at the table by the window. She worked on her Surface Pro, trying to knock off some e-mails during her lunch break. Opposite her sat Lydia Wu, engrossed in her iPad.

They were both legal interns, rapidly rising in the elite legal firm they worked for. While the principals were attending court, they had managed to slip out for lunch.

Lydia quietly, yet excitedly tapped Cynthia's plate with a spoon. Cynthia arched an eyebrow and looked up. With a slight movement of her eyes, Lydia pointed Cynthia to a table to the far left.

Both Lydia and Cynthia loved their Bollywood movies. Lydia thought the two 83 batch gentlemen at that table were Saif and Shahrukh. They were lazily nursing their Tiger beers. 'Shahrukh' suddenly looked towards them and caught Lydia's eye. He nodded with a slight smile. Lydia blushed and looked away. It was noisy in the restaurant.

The two 83 batch gentlemen were used to be mistaken for Bollywood identities in this restaurant. They came here often when they were both in town.

'Saif' was trying to catch Shahrukh's attention. Looked like they were playing a game. Saif was slashing his left forearm with his right arm. Shahrukh was trying to guess, albeit distracted by Lydia.

Saif soon saw what was happening. He signalled a waiter and in signs asked him to invite the two ladies to their table. With practised ease, he slipped him a twenty, as well. It was too noisy to talk. The waiter nodded and went over to the ladies. He tried to tell them what Saif had said. It was too noisy.

So, he repeated the signs Saif had made to him. Actually, he thought he repeated them accurately.

Maybe not...for Lydia stood up and slapped the waiter!

Neither Saif nor Shahrukh looked in that direction again.

Flight to Colombo

He was on a flight to Colombo. As it was a last-minute plan, he could only manage an economy seat. The airline did accommodate him with a window seat. The flight was full of Sri Lankan expats going home for a holiday. Some were stevedores, others construction workers, still others maids and nurses.

He settled in, checked the Wi-Fi, put his iPad mini in the seat pocket in front of him.

A large, oily haired, Sinhalese got into the seat next to him. He had a whiff of overpowering, earthy jasmine scent. It was a 4-hour flight; it had been a long time since he'd flown economy. He flinched but steeled himself for the assault on the senses from the cramped surroundings.

The plane taxied to the runway. People around him stared at the cabin crew performing their safety rituals in awe. He tried to doze off, his neighbour had already established superiority by dominating the shared hand rest and a little territory beyond. He just slouched against the window.

The flight took off. He kept getting poked by his neighbour as headsets went on. Channel surfing on the monitors commenced. The neighbour sought help with his remote; he obliged.

He covered himself with the coarse blanket, positioned a tiny pillow next to the window and tried to sleep.

Sometime later, he became aware of a strong jasmine scent, coconut oiled hair on his chest, and a strange hand crawling up his thigh.

He shrieked!

Pilani/ Gurugram

Chunni Lal removed his starched silk khaadi kurta from the shelf and put it on. The dhobi had brought it in barely an hour ago. It still smelt of charcoal ironing. His jeans had lost some of their crease, but they would have to do. He found his kolhapuris under his bed and wiped the dust off with a rag, before putting them in. He looked in the mirror again and placed a loose lock around his temple back in place. He dabbed some more Old Spice on his cheeks, locked his room and walked out. All his wingees were sleeping after the Sunday lunch. Most were hungover from the Saturday night late night drinks.

He walked up to Meera Bhawan, walking the pavement in the shade, carefully avoiding stepping in any sand. At the gate he had her name announced. As he waited, he itched for a cigarette but resisted the temptation. He checked the crease in his kurta sleeve again. He pondered whether he should fold the sleeves or not. He decided to leave them as they were.

She came out shortly. She looked cool in a starched white salwar cotton kurta. It had little light blue embroidery around her neckline. She wore her hair in a single plait today. She smelt of Ponds Dreamflower talc, as usual. That's what he liked about her; she was simple in her beauty.

They walked past the temple. A few tourists were taking pictures. They went past Vyas. In the upstairs wing, he saw a couple of guys surreptitiously stare at them from behind the pillars.

She was talking about her tests coming up next week, how she had misplaced her notes, etc.

He listened. As they walked, they drew closer. At the corner, where the road turned into C'Not, they turned into Shiv Ganga lawns.

They found a shady, grassy spot and sat down. After some time, he lay down with his head in her lap. The sky had turned cloudy, and a light drizzle had started. There was no shelter nearby, so they decided to ride it out. The sky turned darker, and the rain more intense. They were soon soaked. His kolhapuris were soaked. The cigarettes in his pocket were soaked. Neither the kolhapuris nor the cigarettes would be of any use anymore.

Her white cotton kurta was soaked as well, and her skin was visible as the thin cloth clung to her body. Shyly, she turned away and crossed her arms across her chest. She was shivering in the cold rain. She looked so vulnerable. Slowly, tentatively, gingerly, he reached out to hug her. As he touched her shoulders, she stiffened.

He gripped her shoulders harder. He was breathing hard. His fingers dug into her shoulders.

He felt a strong elbow punch to his tummy. It hurt. He looked around. It was dark. He was in bed.

His wife of 20 years, lying next to him was asking him: why were you hurting my shoulders in the middle of the night?

He slowly got up, and shuffled to the toilet.

Chennai

A deep-seated sigh rose from her full lips. It originated deep within her from her bowels, nay her soul, made its way up her chest and exhaled with a raw, animalistic groan.

He looked at her in awe, dumbfounded by this occurrence. He had known her to be quiet, calm, proper, ladylike ... In fact, too ladylike at times.

They were meeting 3 years after the Silver Jubilee Reunion, at one of those 'luxurious' dhabas on the outskirts of Chennai. He had planned for this for weeks. He picked her up early from her hotel; knowing that the 11 pm Meera Bhawan curfew still applied.

Dressed in a kanjivaram salwar, jasmine in her hair, she could almost have passed for a Chennai kudi. Almost. The Pilani swagger was still there, masked with the now matured 'chalta hai' attitude.

It had all gone well; the drive in his BMW, the special table set up for them, the beer in mud-baked tumblers - until the starter arrived.

Hot steaming samosas served with red sauce and green chutney.

That's when the 'sigh' escaped!

Kufstein, Austria

March, 2016

Ratan Lal was woken up by the persistent buzz of the alarm. It was still dark outside, however the tinkling of brass bells reminded him that the cows were awake and moving in the pastures behind his hotel. He remembered: he had a flight home this morning.

As he threw the blanket off him, he noticed that the other side of his double bed looked ruffled, the pillow a bit askew, the sheet crumpled.

As his mind cleared, it came back to him.

He was here for an industry conference. Having arrived 3 days ago, he was pleasantly surprised by his accommodation in this quiet country town, known for its horses.

At the conference venue, he was checked in by a German volunteer, a student called Cloris. Cloris wore soda glasses, had blonde dreadlocks and sharp features. Ratan Lal saw her eating alone at the conference cafe later that day and joined her. Noticing the vegetarian fare, he was eating, she was curious; they got talking. Her English was rudimentary, Ratan Lal didn't know any German at all; so spontaneous sign language carried the conversation.

He found out that she was a student of Indian politics 1947-2016. Ratan Lal had great insights into politics, without the media hype. Cloris found him a deep source of knowledge, the insights that he gave would have taken her months to research.

It was busy the next day and he didn't see Cloris around.

However, as he entered the conference venue on the last day, Cloris ran up to him, and asked him his plans for the evening. The conference was winding up midday and Ratan Lal had thought about exploring the countryside. Cloris offered to take him around.

They met at two in the afternoon. Cloris had a beat up 1990s Mini. They drove in silence as Ratan Lal took pictures of the countryside on his iPad. There wasn't much conversation; it being fairly difficult to have a sign language conversation when one's hands are on the steering wheel, the other's chunky fingers on the iPad.

Late in the afternoon, she drove into what seemed like a camping ground. Tents were scattered around, people dressed like hippies. Wait! They *were* hippies! She led him to a group where a couple put their smokes away and gave him a hug. They were warm, welcoming...and needed a shower. The stuff they were smoking was quite overpowering. They offered him a 'pipe' and listened attentively as he lectured on Indian politics, Bollywood, economy, cement prices etc.

Around 6pm, as it was getting dark, he looked at Cloris, indicating it was time to go. They stood up, she led him to her car. In the car, she offered him a shawl: her car didn't have heating. Ratan Lal spread the shawl around both their shoulders. The gypsy camp, the smoke, the winding roads made him sleepy, and he dozed. The last he remembered was her pulling his head towards her and resting it on her shoulder as she drove.

He looked again at the pillow next to him. It had a streak of lipstick and some strands of blonde hair.

Bengaluru

Early morning, he went to the bathroom and tightened his white dhoti around him. He looked himself over in the full-length mirror, admiring his bare torso. His idol RajniK would be proud of him.

There was a familiar rumble in the distance. It was too early for the cacophony of car horns and bike beeps.

He climbed onto the commode and peered out of the bathroom window. At the end of the road, where the "LM Rd" sign was displayed, the streetlight illuminated a Harley Rider turning into the street.

Tattooed, bare armed, leather sleeveless jacket, leather pants, hair flowing; she rode to his front gate and revved the Harley.

He dashed out of the bathroom, scrambled down the stairs, opened the gate and sat on the pillion. As she took off with him, she looked back once and said:

"Happy Birthday Machaan."

Dumb Charades around the globe

Pilani, 1985

It was two days after Oasis.

Some of the hangovers were still 'hanging on'. Oasis was always an opportunity for new friendships, short and long-term alliances/ dalliances, binge activities, settling pangas (disputes), starting new pangas and occasionally watching some of the events.

M and S had formed such a casual alliance over the four days as they often found themselves together at some of the more intellectual events, culminating in the dumb charades.

M being from UP, S from TN, the dumb charades worked well. After Engineering Graphics class, they walked up to Sky. M, ever the thorough Lucknavi gentleman, carried both their drafters and paid for the shikhanji and cold coffee.

They settled down under a tree. M dusted off the stray neem leaves and nimbolis with his shawl; then spread it out for them to sit. Gracefully, she collected her yellow parachute/ half-saree ghaghra and perched herself on the shawl and reached out for her drafter and coffee.

M put his kolhapuris at a side and shikhanji in hand, sat down cross legged, smoothing out the front of his kurta over his lap.

They quickly finished their drinks, tossed the remaining crushed ice away and began playing dumb charades. Three slashes on the forearm…three words, one finger up…first word…it went on…

It went on until 6ish when it became dark and they couldn't see clearly, hence began making mistakes.

They picked themselves up, dusted the kurta, parachute/half-sari ghaagra and shawl, collected the drafters and strolled up slowly to their respective messes for dinner.

II.

Washington, 2016

It was the annual CEO charity walk for the homeless of Washington.

The POTUS personally invited CEOs to this walk; 10 laps around the perimeter of the White House, followed by a traditional black tie barbecue in the Southern lawns.

Bubba was invited this year, and though it clashed with business appointments, he decided to do it for the cause.

On a warm spring morning the walk was flagged off by the First Lady. The Secret Service was deployed all around; whilst the POTUS watched from the balcony accompanied by DT and HC who were battling to be the next POTUS.

Bubba wore his BITS 83 black T-shirt, pink shorts and comfortable sneakers, headphones streaming Nusrat Fateh Ali Khan ghazals in his ears. All the walkers had been given navy blue caps with the emblem of the POTUS on the visor.

There was a large media presence, and the event was being beamed live across the globe. It also attracted a large crowd of spectators including tourists.

At about lap 2, Bubba stopped at a drink station where water was being handed out by Hollywood actors who always volunteered at this event. Bubba received his drink from J Roberts of Pretty Woman fame and as he stepped back on the track had a minor collision with another walker. He apologised to her profusely, she waved a good natured: "It's Ok."

As she moved on, Bubba observed that she set up quite a brisk pace and he decided to …. well …keep pace with her. She wore black lycra knee-length tights, a sky blue singlet, a blonde ponytail (which swung with every step), sunglasses, a phone holder band on her upper arm, and white runners with pale blue anklet socks.

Bubba didn't observe much else as he followed her. The sway of her gait and the swishing of her ponytail hypnotised him. A couple of times she looked back and smiled. He didn't know whether she smiled at him; he couldn't see her eyes through her sunglasses.

As they reached lap 9, the other walkers increased pace and it became crowded. He found himself, just behind her, so close that he risked falling onto her. So, he jostled to an opening, walking beside her. As they rounded the final turn, their shoulders brushed each other. She didn't seem to notice. Bubba's heart rate was now rising. She broke into a jog now, he followed shoulder to shoulder.

They crossed the finish line together and received medals from Michelle O.

They walked on together to the change rooms. They tried to talk, but the noise from the spectators was too loud.

She then made one slash with her right hand on his hairy left hand.

Bubba said instinctively: "One word."

She then twirled the middle, ring and little finger of her left hand to him and smiled.

He said: "Bye?"

She nodded and walked away.

III.

Manila, 2017

They met in Manila. Both were on business trips. Batch mates from Pilani; the last couple of years their paths had crossed in different parts of SE Asia.

She was a consultant; he was growing his own global firm acquiring niche customers.

She chose the restaurant. With her newly acquired love for souvlaki and pasta, she chose a Mediterranean joint overlooking the bay.

It had been a long meeting-intensive day for him. He had done a few presentations, answered questions and looked like making some headway with this client. He had spent the past few nights researching for the meeting. Hopefully, they would sign up in the next few days.

He had a long languid shower in his hotel room, downed a couple of San Miguel's from the bar fridge and then changed into his Calvin Klein UW, T-shirt and Chino shorts and sneakers. He dabbed a fair amount of Calvin Klein perfume as well; she had seemed to recognise the scent the last time they met.

He checked his phone. She was already at the restaurant, and not happy waiting.

He left her a quick apologetic message and rushed to the restaurant.

From a flower stall outside the restaurant, he bought a long-stemmed yellow rose. Even though they had known each other for over 30 years, he somehow felt a twinge of apprehension meeting her. There was always an air of slight formality in their first greeting, as she habitually arched her eyebrows and looked at him.

He entered the restaurant with the same air of apprehension and slight nervousness. He looked out to see if he could spot her. She wasn't very tall, but it was early evening and the restaurant wasn't too crowded. He saw her seated by a corner overlooking the bay. She had her back to him. As he approached her; he thought to himself, she hadn't changed much over all these years, the same short wavy hair, the laid-back stance, the ever-sharp mind, the calculated smile, the eyes that bore into him, making him uncomfortable.

He walked up to her and hands behind his back, with extra enthusiasm said: "Hello, Hello!"

She had seen his refection in the window as he had approached. With a slow turn of her head, she put down the glass of Bordeaux she had been sipping and gave him a cool smile. He smiled and gave her the rose. She accepted it and looked at it for some time. Her cheeks were flushed. Could be due to the tropical Manila heat or the glass of Bordeaux or was it just the lighting? He waited.

She put the rose on the side of the table and slashed her right hand on her left forearm.

He blurted: "One word."

She nodded and pointed to the chair opposite her.

He sat.

IV.

University, 2015

He sat in his chamber. This was 'me' time. He asked his secretary to block all visitors, switched off his e-mail and did not take any calls on his desk phone.

His mobile was switched to silent, just in case there was an emergency at home. However, his wife and kids knew about the 'me' time and hadn't disturbed him in his 25 years as a professor.

The walls of the chamber were flush with certificates and accolades he had received through the years. One of the shelves housed printed copies of all the papers he had published. There were a few photographs with other luminaries in his field, a couple of pictures with his BITS batch mates from their Silver Jubilee meet.

Just behind the chair on a hook, hung his jhola (cloth bag) with a few pens, his lunch, a couple of apples, and some scribbled notes. On the back of his chair was his khadi jodhpuri jacket.

He leaned back on his chair and looked at the walls; it was always great to connect with the past. Then he would close his eyes and regurgitate in his mind the latest problem he was researching.

He would draw mental images with his hands in the air to try to link the various bits and pieces.

His face would radiate the emotions of his mental musings; contorted with pain one instant, gleeful another when he found a solution; wry sadness when the dots didn't connect.

Occasionally the hands would weave through the greying luxuriant hair, twirl a lock or two; thump the desk.

This day he rolled up his kurta sleeve; looked at his sinewy forearm, thought about a solo dumb charade, thought about it some more...

...He became aware of a strong sweet familiar fragrance.

There was a hesitant knock on his door.

V.

New York 2016

They finally decided to meet in Central Park.

They had connected a year ago.

Tab had two kids now who studied in NY. He visited them once a year, usually in the summer. Hailing from the warm, sunny, mango orchard banks of the Ganges, he couldn't stand the NY snow and slush.

Sam was single; she had briefly been married to an IITian from Tirunelveli, but the relationship had been suffocating for her. They were living in LA when she broke up.

They had decided to meet that evening as she was travelling through NY. He had seen a few pics on Facebook. Gone was the long hair, the plaits, the half-sari.

He took a cab to Central Park. He chatted idly with the driver, a migrant from Bhatinda. Sensing Tab was not a local, he briefed him on all things to watch out for.

He strolled towards the fountain where they had planned to meet. He passed by a bench, where a man sat engrossed in writing something in a notebook. There was a book (Atlas Shrugged) lying next to him. He looked like a Vijayawada schoolteacher, grey streaked hair, checked shirt, feet neatly folded up tucked under his chin, sandals lying under the bench. The face seemed familiar.

He walked on. He didn't want to be late. He found the fountain. There was an empty bench. However, he was too nervous to sit.

That morning he had had a rather expensive haircut, shaved, worn the cargo shorts his son had given him, with the I (heart) NY black T shirt. The Nike's on his feet were new.

He saw her before she could spot him. It had to be her. Much had changed, but the girlish gait was the same. Elegant in business attire, lugging her business case behind her, stilettos making a determined tap-tap on pathway. The sun filtering down the leaves from those venerable trees, danced through her hair, the shadows creating wavy patterns on her white dress.

She saw him when she was about 25 metres away. A smile broke out on those now bright red lips. With her free hand she gave a gentle demure wave. He walked up, trying to suck in his ample belly. He gave her the bouquet of yellow roses he had been holding onto so consciously. She smiled with genuine delight, moved to give him a hug, and a peck on his cheeks. He stiffened embarrassed by her closeness.

He looked around. No one seemed to care. She saw through his shyness and pointed to a vacant bench. He nodded.

He dusted the bench with his handkerchief before they sat down.

She was so different: glowing cheeks, make-up, changed accent, so confident. Short styled hair, a lone sparkling diamond on a thin chain on her neck. The dress was tight, she obviously trained.

He felt uncomfortable and looked around. She reached out and touched his face and turned it towards her.

She then put her right hand on her left forearm and made three slashes…

It came back to him. "Three words."

One finger: first word; pointed at herself: "I": he blurted.

Three fingers: third word: pointed at him: "You."

He could hear everything now, the breeze, her breath…

He waited for the clue for the second word.

VI.

Dubai

Maltese got out of his chauffeur-driven monogrammed white limousine.

The caparisoned doorman at the restaurant opened the car door for him and saluted. Maltese slipped him a 50 Dirham note.

He entered the restaurant. The manager was at the door to

personally welcome him. He collected Maltese's coat and handed it over to the cloak lady.

Through the dimly lit restaurant, the manager escorted Maltese to a table overlooking the esplanade. Belly dancers in pink sequined headscarves gently swayed across his path sprinkling fresh rose leaves. A live band played a desert melody in the background.

The manager pulled out a chair for Maltese and had him seated. Discreetly a waiter appeared with a champagne bottle in a bucket. After Maltese had seen the label and nodded his approval, the champagne was poured out into a 'Maltese' monogrammed flute. A hookah was also placed on the other side.

The belly dancers positioned themselves discreetly around the table; their swaying mimicking the gentle swaying of the luscious-fruit laden date palms. Their musky aroma filled Maltese's nostrils and he breathed in deeply.

Maltese picked on a sampling of dry fruits placed on his table.

The exec chef then made his appearance with a live lobster on a tray suggesting it as a main to Maltese.

Maltese held his palm up indicating for him to stop. The lobster breathed an audible sigh of relief.

Maltese put his right palm on his left forearm.

The chef said: "One word."

Maltese then spread his fingers to make waves in the air, in sync with the belly dancers.

The chef asked: "Maggi?"

Maltese nodded.

The chef and the lobster trundled back to the kitchen…

VII.

Cochin

It had been very successful career for her so far. Having grown up in a family with deep roots in bureaucracy, she knew the culture very well. She had used this experience in doing the right things, avoiding pitfalls, skirt contentious issues and climb the bureaucratic ladder faster than most people.

Until now…

Mrs Roychowdhary had thought the posting in the Land Tax department in Cochin would be a breeze. Her reputation had preceded her. Smart, intelligent, efficient and with the right political contacts, she was on the rise.

Her first challenge came on the second day on the job. A file had been forwarded to her with a noting by Commissioner Kant. By long practice, she could skim through notes and jot down her own remark: "Approved"/ "To discuss" / "To speak", etc.

However, she couldn't comprehend the language in Kant's noting. The words were genuinely English words, the grammar perfect; only she didn't know what they meant. Quite unlike her usual efficient character, she put the file in a hold basket.

Next day, she 'borrowed' her son's dictionary and brought it to work. She then checked each word, scratched her head, tried to put the words together, scratched some more…finally admitted defeat.

She buzzed her PA and asked for Commissioner Kant to be sent to her office.

Commissioner Kant walked in. He was an intellectual for sure. His aura intimidated her. She stood up to greet him. The PA blinked. Seniors did not stand up to greet juniors!

She sat him down and ordered some tea.

She then, rather sheepishly, asked him to explain his noting on the file. Commissioner Kant looked at the file and said the same things in different words; equally hard for her to comprehend.

There was a stalemate, as she consciously ruffled through the file.

He stared at the ceiling fan, wishing he was in Kufstein or Central Park… anywhere but here.

The tea arrived, served in special china.

Mrs Roychowdhary had arrived at a strategy. She slashed her left forearm with her right palm four times. Commissioner Kant instinctively said: "Four words?"

She 'actioned' the first word. Commissioner Kant said: 'Sepulchral'.

She shook her head and tried a new 'action'. Commissioner Kant said: 'Panjandrum."

Mrs. Roychowdhary gave up. She said she was not well and went home.

Next day she applied for a transfer.

Montana

The six 83 batch 52-year-olds sat around the fire in the log hut sipping Cognac. They watched the flames dance around the fireplace and cast moving shadows on the tiled ceiling.

Their gear was all lined neatly against the wall...sunscreen, bug repellent, boots, GPS trackers, mustard oil dispensers, selfie sticks and ponchos.

They sat in silence...one checking his Nikon SLR, another 'banking' YouTube videos, yet another checking stock prices.

The seventh was outside make a private call to a Swedish camper he had met on the plane. She had sounded lonesome, as they had shared a beer after the plane had landed.

The seventh was excited by his prospects.

In the cabin, the conversation flipped back to times 32 years ago.

They hiked then in chappals, except for Bubba. They had lain in the temple lawns without sunscreen or bug repellent. They did not know about those things then.

Bubba had worn Old Spice on his hikes to Meera. Besides his charm and his Nikes, the Old Spice made him a successful 'hiker'.

Today, a warm glow coloured his cheeks as those memories surfaced again.

The 'seventh' 52-year-old put his satellite phone back in his jhola (cloth bag) and sat on the porch chewing his baccy (tobacco). 20 minutes later, he spewed a stream of baccy juice into a bush, dusted his ample behind and made his way back into the cabin.

Three of his colleagues were snoring, their tummies gently rising and falling in sync. The others looked listlessly through the window at distant stars.

There was an angelic smile on Bubba's face. He was dreaming of happy times.

The group lay together.

Old mate bonhomie.

Leisurely hikes.

Rajasthani-American fusion breakfast.

Sips of local brew.

Early nights.

Age appropriate fun times...

II.

There was a knock on the door.

Hi ...I'm Olivia...I'm from Sweden...I'm a bit lost!

Hi ...I'm Boozo, this is Xai, that's Jogger...and the guy wearing the Stetson is Bubba. Where were you heading?

Some brewery...forget the name.

We're going to one ourselves, tag along if you want. How old are you, Olivia?

I'm 26....why?

We are all 52.

Even Bubba?

Yes.

Oh!

III.

Next morning

Boozo watched Olivia flipping pancakes on the portable stove.

"Nice", he thought and then realised he had said it aloud.

Olivia, turned back and asked "What?"

He said: "I said nice shots, took some great pics this morning."

She said: "Oh!"

Bubba slouching by the railing chewing on a blade of grass, channelling Clint Eastwood, squinted his eyes and glared at Boozo.

He reached into his saddle bag, retrieved a peanut, removed

the shell, tossed one pea into his mouth a la Rajnikanth, and the other into the open mouth of Olivia.

A connection had been established!

Boozo and Xai holstered their pride and passion and walked away into the woods.

IV.

Bubba called the Swedish Embassy.

After a few minutes of conversation and persuasion, he hung up.

He was as puzzled no more....

...Olivia used to be Oliver until about a year ago.

Bubba thought to himself... it was time to find another receptacle for his peanuts.

Away from the crowd he gently massaged his tummy as he lay in his sleeping bag.

Had he really lost a couple of pounds, or was it just an illusion?

He missed his bed at home.

Melbourne

Last night he had watched the cricket.

This morning Rudy went to Victoria market with his partner to buy veggies.

He wore his skinny sky-blue singlet and white board shorts.

As his partner selected bhindis (okra), Rudy waited by the tomato pile.

Getting bored, thinking of his look alike Mitchel Starc, he absentmindedly picked up a juicy ripe tomato and started rubbing it on his 'inner thigh'.

The stall owner Ms Tan walked up to him and asked: What are you doing with that tomato?

Rudy replied: "Reverse Swing!"

Next Week...

Rudy sat on the back of his ute tray selling home grown tomatoes at the Sunday Ferntree Gully farmer's market.

He wore an Akubra hat, a Carlton singlet, out of which poked his hairy arms and chest fluff, tradie shorts and thongs.

On the back of the ute also dozed Lizzie, his kelpie.

An Aussie flag poked out from the antennae (home-made from a coat hanger). The mozzie's buzzed around him as he occasionally reached for a VB stubbie from his Esky.

A few senoritas and sheilas walked past, eyeing his tomatoes and then eyeing him. They haggled. He haggled.

As it was approaching midday; he was aching to join his mates at his local for a cold one and a yarn.

Lizzie was waking up too. Also, the ute tray was becoming uncomfortably hot.

II.

Ajmeri migrated to Australia at the turn of the century with a wife and a couple of toddlers in tow. They soon made friends with another Indian family from Kolkata who lived in the same neighbourhood and had a kid the same age as Ajmeri's daughter. Both the families had a passion for drives and Victoria being a beautiful state (called itself 'the garden state') they did day and overnight trips every other weekend.

Then came Shahrukh!

Well, a BITS batch mate and close friend of Ajmeri came to Melbourne on work and having heard somewhere that Ajmeri was in Australia, looked up the White Pages and found him. He called Ajmeri's home phone, spoke to his wife, she called Ajmeri at work, Ajmeri called the batchmate and after work picked up a six-pack of beer from a bottle shop and landed at his hotel.

They had a reunion on the banks of the Yarra near the CBD and talked and drank late into the evening.

The next time the BITSian friend came to Melbourne he stayed with Ajmeri. And naturally joined Ajmeri and his family on a drive with the family from Kolkata. The lady from the Kolkata family was enamoured of Ajmeri's BITSian friend and thought he looked like Shahrukh Khan.

In the next two years Shahrukh's work brought him to Melbourne every 3 or 6 months. Each time, he stayed with Ajmeri.

After a few more drives around Victoria, the Kolkata lady was more and more convinced they had a Shahrukh look-alike.

A few years later 'Shahrukh' changed jobs.

Sharukh's work (or play) has never brought him to Melbourne since then. Ajmeri and the Kolkata family's kids have grown up and they don't do drives anymore.

III.

The reunion was planned for a Saturday afternoon.

The Non-Veg Mess-Sec (NVMS) had last met the Veg Mess-Sec (VMS) 29 years ago when they both 'managed' the RPA mess.

The NVMS proposed an interesting location for the catch-up. On the outskirts of Melbourne there is a place called the 1000 steps climb. It is exactly what it says it is. 1000 steep steps climbing up 1.5 km on the side of a mountain.

The NVMS did this activity every weekend, both on Saturdays and Sundays, with his wife.

The time proposed was 4.15 pm. The VMS arrived at 4.12 pm and waited. NVMS sent a message saying he would be there in 5 minutes; he arrived at 4.40 pm.

From 4.12pm to 4.40pm the VMS sat in his car, looking at all the fit and healthy types either going to or coming back from the climb. Singlets, shorts, drink bottles, sweat band; VMS was concerned whether he could do it.

When NVMS arrived, he and the VMS greeted each other as if they had met just the day before, rather than 29 years ago.

NVMS was straight into the climb, two steps at a time, without any impacts to his breathing. He didn't even break into a sweat. The VMS was breathing hard about a third of the way and couldn't talk. He asked NVMS to slow the pace down, which he happily obliged. After three short stops, the mountain was conquered: VMS sweating and breathing hard; NVMS was just normal; to add insult to injury he informed VMS that so as not to upset his wife and maintain marital harmony, he had done the climb with his wife earlier that morning. Also, he planned to do it the next morning with her, again.

Anyway, the way down was as steep but more pleasant. As they said bye, they agreed to catch-up again with the other two local batch-mates, this time at the NVMS's house: a more sensible option.

Reykjavik

July 2015

He woke up in a cold sweat in his hotel room in Reykjavik. Had it been a dream?

They had passed a pasture, and despite the cab driver warning him in his Icelandic English, he had stepped out to watch the sheep and take pictures.

He liked sheep. He never missed a chance to visit pastures in the lands he visited. In Hong Kong where he lived there were no pastures; the only sheep he saw were in zoos.

He stood by the fence and looked at them as the autumn breeze ruffled his greying locks. His wiped the condensation off his glasses and took a couple of pictures, which he relayed on WhatsApp.

Some of the sheep strayed towards him. They looked friendly. He jumped over the fence and patted a few. The sheep sniffed at him.

The cab driver honked a warning. He didn't give him any attention.

The sheep rubbed against his feet; soon the whole flock was milling around him. They sniffed around his legs, rubbed against him sensuously, and even tried climbing him.

He looked at the cab driver for help. He was gone!

The sheep tried to trip him to the ground, biting him gently. He was trapped.

Just then over the horizon a KTM Duke 390 appeared with Bengaluru number plates; the grey-haired moustache-less rider sporting an "I am 50" T shirt.

The bike rider, a batchmate stopped by the fence and gave him a hand. He asked him to quickly hop on to the bike.

Looking at his dazed, molested pillion rider he offered by way of explanation: "They are all ewes; they haven't been near a male all summer!"

Hyderabad

After finishing his glorified M Sc Tech Museum Studies degree in 88 and having squandered his time and efforts in the gym, Ajmeri was suddenly left wondering what next. By chance, BITS advertised for Teaching Assistant (TA) roles; Ajmeri applied and got a TA job at a salary of Rs. 1650 per month plus accommodation (bachelor's quarters).

Three months into the role, with no teaching assignment, he was called for an interview in Hyderabad to set up a Science Museum. This was Ajmeri's first trip down south and he wrote to Cookie (83 Mech) who was working in Hyderabad for HCL. Cookie had been a wingee and a close friend. Cookie was there at Secunderabad station to pick Ajmeri up and take him to a flat he shared with some other guys. Ajmeri got the job and then moved to Hyderabad; with some apprehension having lived in Rajasthan all his life.

He was given a good prep by the Hyderabadis in Pilani, including voicing "Naaku Telegu Raadu" (I don't know Telegu) as a standard response to any Telegu queries. However, Hindi worked most times in Hyderabad.

Ajmeri stayed with Cookie and his friends at their flat. The stay there was just an extension of the BITS life. There was one Bengali IITian who was Cookie's colleague in HCL; a couple of sales guys from Vizag, a Cummins diesel mechanic and their friends off and on.

The flat had a huge balcony, equivalent to two bedrooms, where the flatmates sat in the evenings and smoked and exchanged notes. A women's nurse dorm across the street kept them at the balcony more often than not.

Cookie ran the household. He collected a fixed amount every month from the flatmates which paid for rent, breakfast and dinner, plus Saturday night drinks and dinner at the nearby Dolphin Bar and Restaurant. Cookie was also the head home chef, specialising in Dhal and Rajma.

They had a couple of maids, Geeta and her sister Sujata,

who kept the place tidy and looked after the Vizag guys.

About a couple of years into this, Cookie had an interview with WIPRO. Those were the days of HCL-WIPRO sales rivalry, and they asked Cookie what they could offer him to move to WIPRO. Cookie said all he wanted was to go to Delhi (where his family was). The IITian was not impressed as Cookie didn't ask for a raise as part of the deal. Cookie got the job and moved to Delhi.

Ajmeri stayed on in the flat with many people coming and going for another 7 years, until he got married.

II.

Ajmeri had never cooked in his life. So, having the cook in the flat was great. They shared expenses and were equals in roles and responsibilities in the flat. Not in the kitchen though. He was the cook. Period.

He was a good cook. And organised. Each flatmate would be assigned a task: buying ingredients, chopping up onions, washing the rice, rinsing and cleaning up after.

He had this gentle, non-bossy character, but he was the boss in the kitchen.

The cook's favourite dish was Punjabi rajma: a wholesome red kidney beans dish. It was all the flatmates' favourite too. The effort and love in making it was almost spiritual.

When the cook moved to Delhi, Ajmeri and the others had to depend on the cooking skills they had acquired from the cook.

Ajmeri kept in touch with the cook off and on.

One treasures memories of moments spent with nice people, and those who knew the cook, knew he was one of the nicest.

Cookie, the cook fought and lost a battle with cancer a few years ago.

Ajmeri makes rajma every now and then. It is never as good as Cookie made it. It will never be. It doesn't matter. His kids don't care much for the rajma Ajmeri makes. Their mum is a much better cook. So, he ends up eating all of it.

This is the dish Ajmeri enjoys most. It brings back memories of one of the best mates he has ever had.

Kuwait City

2017

The limo stopped in the lobby of the huge glass fronted multinational HQ and the liveried chauffeur quickly opened the door.

The VP stepped out, looking regal in his Saville Row suit, gold rimmed eyepiece and balding pate.

Across the foyer a contingent of immigrant labour was trimming the hedges, when one of them called to the VP: "Sahib!"

He quickly looked and walked away. He didn't know what it was about.

She tried again: "Mallamal Sahib!"

This time he stopped.

She waved: "Sahib, mein Pilani mein aapke room ke peechey ghas katne ka kaam karti thi. Yaad hai aap ko?" (Sir, I used to cut grass behind your room in Pilani, do you remember me?)

The VP embarrassed, quickened his step and marched on without a backward glance.

Later that night...

Ring!

Yuppie here.

Mallamal speaking.

Whatsup?

We are in trouble mate.

Why...stock market crash?

Nah!!! One of the GKWs has identified me. Remember the one we...

Wait, not over the phone!!!

Tihar

2011

The ex-General-Secretary had a dream, maybe a nightmare...

It had been five years since the batch had been incarcerated in Tihar. There were just over 500 of them. They occupied jail number 7.

Five years ago, after a speedy trial in the courts and through the media, they had been sentenced to ten years rigorous imprisonment for a crime that was 'classified'. The main accused Gupta and Noori had never been caught. They had been sentenced in absentia. Rumour had it that Gupta now owned a camel cart business ferrying 'grass' between Gurgaon and Jhunjhunu. Noori had been spotted in the foothills of the Himalayas, people believed.

As for the rest; ConAir and bounty hunters had been busy, collecting the batch from various corners of the globe. Night and day ConAir flights landed at Palam. Bleary eyed, balding, grey haired, shackled men and women arrived in orange prison overalls and were ferried off to jail number 7.

In the five years, they had settled down. They no longer counted the days.

Sheesh had been elected as chief trustee. Jimmy and KV guy had been put into solitary confinement for objecting to the daily cavity searches.

Mallamal had established an undercover business smuggling in and selling Maggi. Muni was the DJ for the prison Akashvani radio station. A few serving professors sat in their cells, composing ghazals.

Kant helped the prison staff with their IT returns (a la Shawshank Redemption). Tani conducted physical training classes for the prison staff.

Vikramsinh was a trustee; he had to count the prisoners in jail number 7 at daybreak and nightfall.

II.

Three years ago, Vikramsinh had successfully petitioned the warden of jail number 7, that all the Sanjays be placed in one cell. This had the desired effect. They were now all called by their last names, easy to do a roll call.

This night Vikramsinh made his rounds of the cells with his iPad, making sure all inmates were accounted for.

As he approached the 'Sanjay' cell, he saw a group had a

small fire going with an earthen pot placed on the fire, in the middle of the cell. Two Sanjays fanned the fire. Mallamal kept watch with a bowl and spoon. The unmistakable smell of Maggi wafted through. They offered Vikramsinh a bowl of steaming hot Maggi as bakshish. He squatted on the floor with his iPad beside him and savoured the delicacy.

As his eyes got used to the darkened corners of the cell, he saw one Sanjay busy with his rope as usual.

(This Sanjay had a friend in the women's cell which was separated from the Sanjay cell by a 20-foot wall. For the past five years, Sanjay had reported each week that his pyjama strings had broken and asked for new ones. He wove these strings into a strong rope. After five years of weaving, he had a rope which was 16 feet long. If anything, this Sanjay was patient).

Meanwhile Vikramsinh picked up his iPad and headed to the Hyderabadi (Little Flower) cell.

III.

As Vikramsinh walked towards the Hyderabadi cell, something on the chaupal (platform) beneath the tamarind tree drew his attention.

There was a lantern burning there and strange shadows emanated from the wavering light.

Gol Guppa was performing his birthday-eve rituals.

Dressed in a yellow silk kaftan with red dragon print, pink rouge on his cheeks, he was going through some intricate tai-chi motions. The quiet of the night was broken by the gentle swish of the silk and his graceful moves.

Mesmerised, Vikramsinh looked over at the wall of the ladies' cell where the elongated shadows created ghostly figures. He shivered and broke into a cold sweat.

He saw something radiant gleaming over the wall. Looked like cat eyes. Could be humans, maybe the ladies watching the Go Guppa dance… Vikramsinh shivered some more and gripped his iPad tightly.

Gol Guppa paused.

He reached towards the trunk of the tamarind tree. From

the crevice of one of the branches, he brought out a bottle of Old Monk, had a long sip, sprinkled some of the rum around the chaupal; and resumed his tai-chi.

From previous experience, Vikramsinh knew this would go on all night. It still felt eerie.

Vikramsinh thought he would wish Gol Guppa tomorrow on his birthday.

He walked on, stepping through the shadows….

IV.

In a corner of the mess in jail number 7, there was a small disused wooden crate placed. A long-haired, bearded gentleman, ex-Nagpur, dressed in a double-breasted suit with a burgundy cummerbund stood with a leg placed on the crate,

A violin was tucked under his chin, and his hand deftly wielded the bow, gliding it sensuously over the strings. As if touched by angelic feathers, the strings brought out a soulful melody "ek pyaar ka nagma hai..."

V.

There was a change in government and the new home minister decided to grant amnesty to the batch.

There was speculation in the media that the real reason behind the amnesty was possible exposure of links between powerful lobbies and some of the inmates through the Panama Papers.

There was general rejoicing and much backslapping in Jail Number 7.

The mess served raisin Pulao, mutter-paneer and cassata ice-cream to mark the occasion.

The recently turned 49-year old Gupta, now no longer under cover, organised a fleet of Volvo buses to transport the inmates to a holding location, a farmhouse in Faridabad. The local paparazzi took up positions in the trees along the boundaries of the farmhouse.

The open-air tube well attracted most attention as the inmates had their first proper bath in years.

The international recruiters dealing in CEO/ CFO/ CIO roles descended in droves into Delhi.

Share prices restabilised around the globe.

The Sanjay had brought his yet-to-be-completed rope with him as a memento. He packed it in a Calvin Klein shopping bag and tearfully bid farewell to his lady friend before boarding his personal Lear jet.

Vikramsinh checked each inmate out collecting their forwarding addresses.

With a heavenly, beaming smile, the G-Sec dreamt on…

Gurugram

2017

They were near the Hero Honda chowk.

He had called his driver early that day. It had rained all night. He hadn't slept well. As he had tossed and turned, his wife thought maybe it was work worries again. She had turned away and dozed off. He had a careful shave, wore his new shirt, checked for any signs of grey in his moustache. He had his usual cornflakes and milk for breakfast. The driver had collected his bag. They had driven off.

They had collected her from the hotel in Gurugram.

She was fresh as a daisy, hardly changed in the 30 years since he had seen her. He had seen more recent pics on FB. Awkwardly they shook hands, as he led her to the car. His driver, though discreet and loyal, couldn't hide his curiosity completely. Their eyes met in the rear-view mirror occasionally, the driver hurriedly looked away.

She was quite loud and friendly and full of questions. She sat close; he was slightly uncomfortable at her closeness, especially with the driver keeping a stealthy eye. He should have given the driver a day off and driven himself.

An hour or so later, he noticed they hadn't made much

progress. The roads were flooded, traffic crawled; his normally calm driver was giving the horn a workout.

It was planned as a day trip. He had plans for the time at the resort. This delay wasn't helping.

She got a call on her phone. She shyly excused herself, shifted towards the window and spoke softly. She told whoever was on the phone that she was on her way to a business meeting.

He put a message on WhatsApp to his batch mates about the traffic jam. Advice poured in from around the world. The Singapore twins were more practical; whilst one suggested beer, the other spoke about being wary of nature's calls.

Suddenly he wanted to go to the loo.

She had finished her call and moved in close again.

Something became agitated within him; it wasn't just the need to visit the loo. He shuffled restlessly in his seat. He looked longingly at the water bottle in her hands.

Helsinki

2015

The pink stretch Hummer stopped in front of the golden SAS Towers in downtown Helsinki.

The tall Masai doorwoman hurried to the Hummer door and held it open for him to step out. He was returning from his early morning golf rounds. He had been in peak form this morning.

As he always did, he stopped and looked at this impressive structure, one of the finest in all of Europe according to some. The intertwined SAS logo ran across the length of the frontage.

In his red polo top and khaki chinos, he walked up to his personal lift accompanied by the doorwoman.

As the lift noiselessly deposited him to his penthouse suite cum office, his secretary Toni received him with a cup of coffee.

As usual he walked straight up to the open-to-sky jacuzzi, whilst Toni perched on a stool at his feet discussed his appointments, both business and personal, for the day.

Today, Toni was confused.

An envelope had arrived from the hotel across the street

addressed to him. Inside was just an old dried leaf, a kind of leaf Toni had never seen before.

Toni showed it to him. His face changed colour and he nearly jumped out of the jacuzzi. His heart racing, he hardly heard Toni.

It was a neem leaf!

Memories came flooding back.

30 years ago, he had said goodbye to Mila at the Meera Bhawan gates. Holding back tears, and heartbreak, they had exchanged neem leaves to keep as mementos. He had lost touch with her since then.

He asked Toni to hand him his monogrammed purple bath robe. He then dashed to his desk and found the leaf she had given him.

Tears welled up in his eyes. Toni handed him some tissues, not understanding why a dried leaf could make this tycoon cry.

He quickly changed into a suit, groomed his hair and walked himself to the hotel across the street.

From her window on the fifth floor Mila watched him and waited for the knock on the door...

Guwahati

In the winter break of '87, Ajmeri visited Guwahati and Shillong with his North-East batch mates. He stayed mainly with Tall Dutta but did spend one night at Short Dutta's place.

At that time Ajmeri was at the prime of body building (in his own mind) and had acquired a dietary habit of a few raw eggs pre breakfast each morning. In his limited knowledge of weight training nutrition, the raw eggs and a litre of milk with a generous dose of Protinex was the ultimate solution.

So, the night before sleeping at Short Dutta's house, Ajmeri made sure they had enough stock of eggs (by the way it was 4 eggs when he was not in training; 6 eggs when he was).

The next morning, he woke up before Short Dutta. Short Dutta's mum was awake with the eggs and a glass. She asked Ajmeri whether he'd prefer them to be cooked for a change. He said no. She watched in fascination as he broke the eggs and put them in a glass and then gulp them down in one go. He then went on to the terrace to await Short Dutta rising from his sleep, whilst he breathed in the crisp Guwahati air. Short Dutta had some delightful neighbours.

He left Short Dutta's house later that morning and has never seen his mum since.

27 years later…

Ajmeri spoke to Short Dutta for the first time after leaving Pilani. Short Dutta is now based in the Middle East. After detailing to Ajmeri the loves of his life - his stable of Porsches, his wife and kids - he mentioned that a month back he had visited his mum who now lives in Kolkata.

One night as he sat with his mum looking at Facebook (as you do) ...Short Dutta scrolled to one of Ajmeri's posts with a picture of him; she exclaimed: "Isn't this the guys who drank the raw eggs?"

What a memory!

London

The Palace had been decked up for the occasion. The ceremonial hall had been prepared; the throne placed in the centre of the hall.

A red carpet had been laid leading to the throne. The queen entered in a procession, her corgis and Prince Philip following at a respectful distance.

The crown was placed on her head, and a purple cushion at her feet. The corgis sat at her feet; Prince Philip took his seat with the courtiers.

600 years of British history and tradition went into the pomp, splendour, costumes and ceremony.

The Royal Crier announced the special guest. The guest had been driven in a six-horse carriage, with page boys perched behind him.

He was wearing the traditional chorno & kediyu, his staff

in the crook of his arm as he waved to the crowds lining the streets.

He entered the ceremonial hall, a picture of grace, aura of power.

Kate and Pippa standing in the side wings behind the purdah giggled like teenage girls; they would seek a selfie with him later.

The ceremony was being beamed live across the world, with a live feed on the BITS 83 batch website.

He bowed before Her Majesty. She stood up. The corgis wagged their little tails in anticipation.

A sword was handed to the queen. She tapped him on each shoulder with the sword…and said:

"Rise, Sir Anar!"

II.

Sir Anar had been summoned to Buckingham Palace. The Queen wanted to meet him within the hour.

He had been having a lazy lunch in a small and discreet Mehsana cuisine restaurant with his batch mate and fellow Londoner, Duke Rumpy.

They had just finished, and lit up their pipes by the fireside, when Harry from the Palace arrived bearing the summons.

Sir Anar, read the note, passed it on to Duke Rumpy, who nodded.

Harry had brought the Royal carriage. The three walked down to it. Duke Rumpy was attired in his latest fancy these days. He had been frequenting 221, Baker St and had adopted the dressing habits of its esteemed ex-inhabitant. Long grey coat, top hat, oak-wood walking stick and a briar pipe in hand, he exhibited grandeur.

Sir Anar, as was his wont, had settled the bills with a standard tip to the waitress.

On the way to the palace, Harry sat quietly, respectfully.

Arriving at the palace, they were ushered in quickly to the Queen's library, where they met Her Highness, Pippa and PM June.

They bowed to each other. Duke Rumpy took a spot by an open window and lit his pipe.

Sir Anar arched his left eyebrow. PM June explained that they were having trouble choosing a cabinet and needed Sir Anar's political judgement and advice.

This was what Sir Anar enjoyed.

He asked Pippa to set him a cushion in a corner and get him a lemonade. He sat on the cushion, cross legged, whilst Pippa squatted besides him, fanning him with an antique 16th century Japanese fan.

For the next thirty minutes, he was busy making calls around the world.

He then asked Pippa to write up his list of ministers.

She wrote diligently. The fate of many a politician was being decided in the strokes of that pen.

Pippa helped Sir Anar back to his feet. Duke Rumpy dusted his pipe in the geranium pot by the window and they both walked away.

Duke Rumpy's walking stick tapped a steady beat in the corridor.

Pilani

2018

She woke up early that Saturday morning, even before the blue-dialled radium Favre-Leuba alarm clock could go off. She was excited. She sat up in bed, tied her luxuriant hair in a bun, cast off the sheet covering her, smoothed out the nightie and rolled her legs off the bed.

The purple packet of Charms was on the desk. She reached out, tapped one cigarette out expertly, put it to her lips, grabbed a pale green lighter from the floor and lit up. The lighter fluid was nearly over, she would need to get it refilled at her next trip to Nutan.

Cigarette dangling at the corner of the mouth, she walked up to her cupboard and selected her clothes for the event. She had heard he was a slick dresser, in fact a brand ambassador; she had to dress right to make an impression.

Showered, dressed, elegant make-up done, she cycled to the Audi.

ManG was in charge of the stage setting for the book signing. His ruffled hair, smudged glasses, crumpled kurta, indicated he had put in an all-night effort.

AJ, with his signature hat, was setting up his cameras at vantage points. KV guy and Naren had setup a ThumsUp and allied products stall close by.

She joined the already long queue of autograph hunters. Fifteen minutes before the author's arrival, the head of the reception committee had been dropped off in his Amby. He stood now, one handing clutching his dhoti, the other a bouquet of flowers.

A buzz was heard in the distance, which grew noisier by the minute. An Augusta-Westland helicopter circled the campus once, before descending onto a specially built temporary helipad.

The door opened, and squeals of delight went up from the queue of autograph hunters. Sauvé, 'debonair', ex-BITS, the renowned author strode to the stage, nodding at the crowds through his aviators. After receiving his bouquet and a quick chat with ManG, he took his place behind the table. A special satin-covered, embroidered mooda had been placed for him.

As she reached him, her heart began to beat faster. She popped a mint in her mouth, touched up her lips with some lipstick, and with a demure smile asked him to sign a copy of his book.

Without looking up, he asked for her name to write on the cover. She didn't answer.

Slightly annoyed, he looked up at her.

Time stood still.

He looked at her glowing cheeks, the luxuriant coiffured hair, the slightly parted lips, the naughty challenging look in her kohl lined eyes.

The 'Author' blushed...

Southern United States

2018

There was an annual music festival in Delhi called Bindaas BITSians...attended by senior BITS alumni.

However, this meet caused an incident in a southern capital in the United States.

The CEO walked briskly into his office, loosened his tie, folded his sleeves, and looked at the city through the windowpanes of his penthouse office.

The stately, prim, spinster Mrs Radcliffe entered the room with a glass of chai and placed it on his desk.

The CEO had moved here a couple of years ago after setting the industry alight in Europe. He had brought along with him the trusted 83-year-old Mrs Radcliffe.

This morning Mrs Radcliffe looked a bit angry.

She said there was a call from a Bhalu from Delhi inviting the CEO to a musical program.

The CEO said that he might go.

Mrs Radcliffe said that she had already declined on his behalf. He asked, why?

She said in her acquired American accent, hyphenating the program name ...Well sir, the program is called 'Bind-ass' something! I didn't think you were into that sort of thing...

The CEO coloured up and shook his head.

As Mrs Radcliffe stepped out of the office, she looked back briefly.

It was clear she wasn't convinced...

NCR

2017

He was having his afternoon siesta. The autumn afternoon was cool, gentle breeze rustled through the yellowing neem branches, cascading a few leaves onto the statues in his garden, some settling on him as he lay in the hammock.

His French wife looked at her watch and started preparing afternoon tea.

She watched in fascination at the gentle lift and drop in his tummy as he snoozed.

Today he had a special smile on his face...

He was dreaming, recollecting, reminiscing.

Another time, 30 years ago, an autumn Sunday afternoon. He was lying down in Sky, his head nestled in P's lap. P sang soft verses in Bengali. He had had a heavy lunch and was happy.

She usually tied her hair in pigtails. That day she had left it open, as she had washed her hair in the late morning. The damp smell of shampoo, strands of her hair brushing his face; he had opened his eyes and saw the sun peer through her tresses...

Just then he was woken up from his reverie by his wife: "Mon cheri chai."

She looked at the expression on his face. Being French, she knew the look.

She ran!

Shepherds

A few years ago, the principal shepherd had been instrumental in collecting these sheep. It had been 25 years since they had dispersed from Pilani to various corners of the globe. He had collected them for the batch silver jubilee meet.

They were different now. Some grey, some portly, some still 'hot', some sadly missing...

There were Professors, Tax Collectors, Bridge builders, CEOs, CIOs, CFOs, Business Owners, Teachers...

He collected them and gathered them in his pasture. He established the pasture on Google Groups. The sheep were excited to see each other; they shared stories, opinions, poems, cartoons, dog stories, duck stories, love stories; some real, some imaginary.

The shepherd had help. He had a silent but strong co-shepherdess and another shepherd who built the fences and went back to the void space of nirvana once the sheep had been collected.

Then came WhatsApp, and some of the sheep saw that the grass was greener on the neighbouring WhatsApp pasture. This new pasture was challenging for some in more ways than one. Rules were established, broken; some left the pasture, rejoined, left again and then didn't care much about leaving or joining.

A new shepherd was appointed for the WhatsApp group, and the fence was opened for the sheep to cross over to the new pasture. A few were excited, others reluctant.

The shepherd continues keeping watch on the Google pasture

The shepherdess keeps watch too…

It is very quiet.

II.

The old pasture has become a resting place; a place to chew the cud. The sheep rarely interact anymore, just an occasional soft bleat. The grass grows around them; their merino coats are turning grey...

Gone are the days of passionate, engaged discussions; reminiscing, poetry, videos, cartoons and occasional mid-life anxiety issues.

Even the Principal shepherds now rarely walked up to the fence... just to see if the sheep were behaving. They need not bother. Inertia rules.

III.

Late one night, at the fence between the two pastures, under the cover of darkness; there was a clandestine rendezvous.

There had been a discussion in the WhatsApp pasture about some of the sheep who had been snoozing in the Google pasture and didn't venture into the WhatsApp pasture anymore.

Some alluded that the shepherdess was the cause of it.

It was clarified through a media release (from unknown sources); that the shepherdess had not been responsible; she had been a great sport right through, pedas (milk sweets) were offered as a peace offering.

IV.

It was a clear night. The first stars had appeared at about 8 pm. The pesky crows had flown to their trees. There they sprayed a digested and processed ejection of their day's scavenging on the unsuspecting sheep gathered under the trees.

As was their ritual, they expended their energy on a vocal cacophony, before pulling their heads under their wings and melting into the darkness of the night.

The sheep meanwhile had moved to the open meadows and rested in groups; their warm breath mingling into the cool evening breeze.

The shepherds gathered around a small fire on a hillock overlooking both pastures; wrapped in their shawls, keeping a wary eye out for predators.

Both pastures had a small area cordoned off. At about 11 pm, two of the shepherds gently coaxed the ewes into the cordoned off areas. They did this every night, except for one month in a year, which was mating season.

This night, after the ewes had been separated, the shepherds settled into keeping watch, as usual.

In the WhatsApp pasture, there was some movement. One of the sheep slowly wandered towards the ewe enclosure. He let out a soft bleat. Hearing it, one of the ewes looked around at her sleeping companions and shuffled to the fence.

They met there and for some time stood side by side, shoulders touching each other through the gaps in the fence.

The male then moved his head towards the ewe's nose. They rubbed their warm, moist noses against each other.

V.

The first rays of a new sun splashed gently across the meadows. The morning dew had settled on the grass. The sheep due to their thick coats were impervious to the dew.

They lazily started munching the dew laden grass. It was delicious.

The shepherds on the hillside beat out their fire. It had been a cold night and they had run out of firewood in the early hours. As usual, they had improvised and used the pages of Debs to keep the fire going.

Wasps of smoke were visible from the village nearby as the house folk cooked up breakfast. The shepherds, tired after their night watch, awaited relief.

On the twisted path from the village, pranced gaily the shepherdess. She was always bright and bubbly in the mornings. Wearing a colourful ghagra, shiny choli, lac bangles all the way up to her upper arms she ran up to the herd. Her anklets tinkled in the silence of the pastures.

After a quick glance at the Google pasture, she released the ewes from their night confinement.

With excited bleats, they ran to join the males.

Picking up a black lamb from the WhatsApp pasture, she cuddled it and settled down under the banyan tree.

The shepherds trudged back to the village ...

VI.

The Principal shepherd wasn't happy!

He sat on the hillock, holding his ceremonial gold plated, ruby inlaid, ivory staff under the ancient English oak overlooking his peaceful pastures, with an expanse of well-fed sheep, and ruminated.

Along with the shepherdess, he had kept the sheep in check, and watched as they fattened. Occasionally they would fight, he would step in and with a royal stare return them to order.

Excepting the pesky, annoying Aussie black sheep, they generally behaved.

He looked around for the shepherdess. She sat on the twin hillock away from him... From a distance, he saw her; tried to read her eyes.

She looked away.

He wasn't happy!

Reminiscing...

His heart started pumping as he rounded the bend and he could see the Meera Bhawan gates. He felt conscious as he took the last few steps, as if all the eyes of the world were on him.

He was freshly showered and shaved, his clothes washed and pressed; the creases still prominent and visible. Not a strand of hair out of place.

The girls walking in and out of the hostel glanced at him from the corner of their eyes. He was a new visitor. His self-consciousness was obvious. A couple of the girls giggled. How rude, he thought to himself.

He announced himself to the gatekeeper and then waited under a tree, trying to merge into the background.

Another couple was there, saying never-ending goodbyes. Then with a promise to meet the next day and a lingering handshake, the guy walked away, lighting a cigarette as he went.

He turned his gaze back to the gate, waiting for her to appear. His nervousness grew. What would he say? Was he overdressed?

A rickshaw passed by, the driver purposefully ringing his bell, teasing him. He let out a swear word, watching the rickshaw go around the bend.

Then a sweet waft of jasmine drifted towards him. A warmth came near him. He turned slowly. She was there. An amused tinkle in her eye, slight colour in her cheeks. She looked so much more relaxed than when he sat beside her in class.

He blushed and then, quickly, his mask of masculinity and confidence came back on. They walked to Blue Moon, a restaurant on campus. She was full of innocent joy, even playful. His nervousness and consciousness melted away. They walked as friends, as a couple.

30 years on, he still remembers, remembers vividly...

■ ▨

Oasis 1987

Skylab 1985

Institute 1986

Temple 1985

Shiv Ganga 1985

CPSIA information can be obtained
at www.ICGtesting.com
Printed in the USA
BVHW090855011120
592280BV00027B/1653

9 781645 601265